AF425393

Fireworks & Felons

Holiday Cozy Mystery

B I Skinner

Contents

Chapter 1

"What in blazes?" I muttered sleepily when the sharp wail of sirens woke me from a deep slumber. I had dreamed I was playing hide-and-seek with George Washington on the iconic Pearl Street Mall in Boulder, Colorado. But why? Who had dreams about George Washington? I bet it was due to the community's preparations for the upcoming 4th of July Festival, which was only a week away. It was a wildly popular event every year, and this year was the 100th anniversary.

According to the sliver of sunlight peeking through the bedroom curtains, dawn was breaking over Boulder, but the obnoxious blare of sirens shattered the tranquility of what would typically have been a quiet Saturday morning. Still groggy, I reluctantly stirred from my slumber and reached out to silence my alarm clock when I realized that the clock wasn't the problem. What *was* the deal with all the sirens?

As an army veteran and retired Boulder police detective, I rarely needed to set an alarm clock. My adopted dachshund Scooby typically woke me with eager kisses, excited to run outside before breakfast. But this morning, Scooby was still sound asleep as well. When I stirred, he did too, his ears perking up at the harsh sounds.

"Whatever it is, it's serious," I told Scooby. I hoped it wasn't anything *too* serious. I knew firsthand how sirens often signaled a life-changing event for someone and hoped all involved would be okay. "What do you suppose it's about?" I grumbled, rubbing the sleep from my eyes. With a soft whine, Scooby sprinted down his special ramp and ran from the room, his toenails clicking on the hardwood floor as he dashed down the stairs and toward the back door.

Whether I wanted to or not, that meant it was time to get up and start the day. I pulled on my worn but beloved navy blue plaid robe and slid into my tan bedroom slippers. I stopped briefly to rub my arthritic knee - a leftover reminder of the time I tackled a streaker who ran onto Folsom Field during a University of Colorado football game (boy, did that video go viral!) - before venturing downstairs to let Scooby out into the backyard to do his business and investigate any new smells that popped up in his yard overnight.

Shuffling into the kitchen, I started the coffee and, with a sigh, set about preparing breakfast, mindful of my doctor's annoying warnings about cholesterol. In my feeble attempt to adhere to healthier habits, I opted for oatmeal and a handful of blueberries. My granddaughter Ellie was always on my case to eat better, too.

"Would it kill you to add a vegetable to that meal?" she'd scold.

"It might!" I'd retort.

Ellie was a student at the University of Colorado, and my excuse for staying in the house I shared with my wife Lisa, the love of my life, who passed away three years ago from pancreatic cancer. My daughter Olivia, who lived in Miami, nagged me repeatedly to move there. "I'm fine where I am," I told her at least once a week. "Besides, Ellie needs someone to look after her." That was my excuse anyway, and I stuck to it.

After Scooby finished what he needed to do in the backyard, he scratched on the door and then bolted for the bowl of kibble I put out.

"Let's see if there's anything good on TV, Scoobs," I told him while pointing the remote at the set in the living room.

The screen flickered to life, revealing a shocking scene that sent a jolt through my body. Several floats for the 4th of July Festival—a place of laughter and community only yesterday—were on fire. My heart raced as I spotted at least three floats, each a product of countless hours of devoted craftsmanship, reduced to smoldering ruins. That explained the sirens.

I leaned forward, squinting at the images as if I could make sense of the disarray by looking harder. The disbelief was immediate, and the pang of loss was sharp. Those weren't just decorations; they were symbols of our community's spirit and unity. My hand unconsciously gripped the remote tighter, my knuckles whitening.

"What on earth?" I cursed, unable to comprehend what I saw, when my phone rang. It was Sammy, a fellow veteran, owner of the Veteran's Hearth Bar, and my best friend.

"Hey," I grunted.

"Hey," he grunted back. "You watchin' the news?"

"Yep."

"What happened?" he asked.

"Dunno," I replied. Yes, we were men of many words. "Lightening?" I suggested.

"Maybe," he said. "Or someone could have dumped a cigarette butt nearby."

I nodded. "Good possibility. People are careless." When my phone beeped, I glanced at the screen. It was Jack.

"Hang on a sec," I told Sammy. Jack is another close friend and a fellow veteran who's in a wheelchair and just got a service dog from the VA. He's also an Intellectual Property Rights lawyer for one of the most prestigious firms in Boulder.

"Hey," I said.

"Hey. You watchin' the news?"

"Yep," I grunted again.

"My buddy with the Boulder Fire Department said it's arson," he informed me.

I stared at the phone in disbelief, the gravity of the situation sinking in. "Arson? Are they sure?" The thought of a person carelessly flicking a cigarette butt too close to the floats was one thing, but someone deliberately destroying our work was another.

"They're sure. They found an empty bottle of lighter fluid from Maginni's Hardware under one of the floats. But they don't want to release the news to the public yet. They're worried it will cause widespread panic."

Jack's next words were drowned out by Scooby barking maniacly at the doorbell. I've been awake for less than an hour, and the day has been nothing but bedlam. What next?

"Jack, I'll have to call you back. Someone is at the door," I explained over the cacophony of dachshund barking.

"What?" Jack asked.

"I'll have to call you back--"

"Is someone at your door?" he said.

"Yes. I... oh, forget it." I grumbled, hanging up on him. He'd figure it out eventually.

I was surprised to see Detective Laura Rodriguez through the peephole. What could she want at this hour? Detective Rodriguez was a young (younger than me, anyway) detective in Boulder, and while we maintained a cordial relationship, we butted heads on the regular, too. She was a first-rate detective who, I suspected, saw me as a meddling old retiree who would make her life easier if I'd stick to fishing and wood carving and stay out of her way.

"Detective Rodriguez," I greeted when I opened the door. Her dark hair was pulled back into a neat ponytail, and she wore a sharp gray suit with a white blouse. Despite her short stature, she commanded a formidable presence, intimidating even the biggest men with her sharp wit and no-nonsense demeanor that left no room for doubt or challenge.

"Detective O'Sullivan," she said with a brief smirk as she eyed the robe and slippers I forgot I was wearing. But the smirk was quickly replaced with a sharp gaze and firm set to her jaw. Uh oh. She was here on business. I was immediately reminded of the last time she showed up unexpectedly on my doorstep when I may-have kind-of sort-of kept a custom key I found at a crime scene hidden from her for longer than I should have. Or, as she put it, that I shouldn't have hidden at all. Thankfully, in the spirit of Christmas, she forgave me and made me swear I'd never do it again.

Standing on my porch, Detective Rodriguez wasn't the only thing that greeted me on this odd June morning. Behind her, Boulder had awakened in all its serene glory; the early sun painted the Flatirons in hues of orange and pink while the lush greenery of my neighborhood shimmered with dew, not yet evaporated by the hot summer sun that was sure to come later. It was a picture of peace that I was privileged to view every single day, and it never got old. Yet my daughter still thought I should move to Florida. No way.

"May I come in?" she asked.

"Of course," I said, opening the door further.

When Scooby realized who was at the door, he launched into a comical dachshund dance for her, partly excited that she might have a treat and partly excited that we had company.

"Hey there, Scooby!" she cooed, bending down to give him a friendly chin rub.

"I'd offer your breakfast, but the best I can do today is oatmeal and blueberries," I told her regretfully.

She smiled briefly while tucking a lock of stray hair behind her ear. "That's okay. I'm actually here on official business."

"What's this?" I asked when she handed me a slip of paper encased in an evidence bag. I scanned the scrawled, crude note written on a scrap of thick, creme-colored paper.

This is only the beginning. Cancel the 4th of July Festival, or the fireworks won't be the only explosion in town. You got lucky last time O'Sullivan. It won't happen again.

Chapter 2

A cold shiver ran down my spine as I scanned the crudely scrawled message.

"You assume this was directed at me," I told the detective, who responded only with an icy glare. "Surely there must be tons of O'Sullivan's out there, right?"

Detective Rodriguez' ongoing gaze told me everything I needed to know.

Try as I might to pretend the note couldn't be directed at me, it obviously was. The words were stark, threatening, and deeply personal—a dare to intervene and a warning that I was already a target. I clenched my jaw as I held the note, my fingers pressed into the evidence more forcefully than necessary.

"So it *was* arson," I muttered more to myself than the detective. The idea that someone would deliberately set the community's hard work ablaze, risking lives for some unknown purpose, set a fire of its own in my belly.

"When you ask it like that, it tells me you already had your suspicions," Rodriguez said.

I exhaled forcefully. "Jack told me someone in the fire department tipped him off. But this makes it official?" I asked, locking eyes with her.

Her nod was grim. "Aside from the note, the fire looks like a professional job. Not just kids goofing around." The weight of what we're up against pressed down on me. The town's safety and the peace of this festival we've celebrated for 100 years were at risk. Even as I still wanted to deny this could have anything to do with me, my mind raced through potential suspects and motives. Who could it be?

"Any fingerprints?" I asked, holding the note up to the light as if I could detect something that way. "And Jack said they found an empty bottle of lighter fluid at the scene."

"No fingerprints so far, but we'll see what the boys in the lab have to say," Rodriguez responded.

In the quiet of my living room, the tension was almost palpable as Detective Rodriguez stared at me. The morning light filtered through the blinds, casting long shadows that underlined the gravity of the situation. "Can you think of anyone who would do this?" she asked, her voice steady, her brow furrowed in concern. "And why single you out?"

I rubbed the back of my neck, feeling the weight of years and memories pressing down on me. The room felt suddenly colder, or maybe it was just the chill of old ghosts stirring. "I've put away a lot of bad folks in my time. Could be any one of them holding a grudge."

I flashed back to last night when we were working on the float for Sammy's bar with plans to finish it today. We had so much fun, and all was right with the world. Our laughter and jokes mixed with the sounds of hammers, drills, and classic rock music blaring from a nearby radio. Ellie darted around the float with paintbrushes, adding artistic touches to the signage, while Scooby, decked out in a miniature Veterans Hearth Bar bandana, trotted between us, his tail wagging as he looked for snacks and head rubs. I was relieved this morning when I saw it wasn't *our* float that burned, but then I felt guilty for even thinking that. If someone was threatening the town, the floats were meaningless.

Rodriguez nodded and tapped her finger against the note as if it needed emphasizing. "This," she tapped harder, "mentions you getting lucky in the past. Does that ring any bells? Something specific that might have triggered this?"

I closed my eyes and let my mind drift back to cases that didn't sit right, the unresolved edges of investigations where justice felt more like a compromise. "A few come to mind," I told her. "There was one case," I started, hesitating while the edges of that old memory sharpened, "a series of arsons we linked to a repeat offender, but he disappeared and hasn't been heard from since."

Rodriguez' interest peaked, and her posture stiffened. "Could he be back?"

"Maybe? I don't know. And why now?" I pondered out loud, the idea settling like lead in my stomach. My gaze fell to the note again, the words taunting me from the paper.

"I'll increase patrols around your neighborhood just to be on the safe side. And would you be willing to come down to the station later today to discuss some potential suspects? Anyone you could think of who might fit the profile of an arsonist with a grudge against you. I could have my assistant Ronnie pull some old files for you if you think that would help jog your memory."

I started to tell her I was working on the float today, but clearly, I was not. And here I thought retirement meant I didn't have to go to the station anymore. Not for work anyway. "Sure, I suppose I could. And while you're at it—" I started...

"I'll also increase patrols around your granddaughter's neighborhood," she added.

A wave of relief washed over me, lightening the burden of worry just a bit.

"I'll warn you right now, O'Sullivan, because of this, the mayor is seriously considering canceling the 4th of July Festival, and he's asked the police department to weigh in on the decision."

"What? No! He can't do that! It's a tradition. The town will be heartbroken. People look forward to this all year. And especially this year with the 100th anniversary."

"We can't risk the community's safety. Surely, you, of all people, know that. Unless we can catch the arsonist, I have to agree with the mayor. The 4th of July Festival should be canceled."

The concern in her eyes mirrored the tightness I felt in my chest. It wasn't just a meaningless threat—it was a dark echo from my past, resurfacing when I least expected it.

But I stood firm, my voice rising involuntarily. "We can't let some crackpot bully us into canceling the festival, Detective. It's more than just a celebration; it's part of the community. It's the 100th anniversary! If we back down now, we're not just disappointing all those families, we're letting fear dictate our lives." My words carried a mix of frustration and conviction, emphasizing the importance of standing strong in the face of threats to preserve a cherished community legacy.

I listened as Detective Rodriguez laid out her reasoning, her tone steady but firm. "I get where you're coming from,

Howie, and I understand how much this festival means to everyone," she began, while her eyes met mine with a sincerity that told me she wasn't taking this lightly. "But we have to consider the safety of the town first. If we can't catch this guy in time, canceling the festival might be our only option, even if it upsets people. It's a tough call, but I'd rather have disappointed folks than dead folks."

"I'll do everything I can to ensure that doesn't happen," I vowed.

Chapter 3

"I'll be in touch later today, " I promised Detective Rodriguez just before shutting the door behind her; the click of the latch echoing in the quiet entryway. I paused and leaned against the heavy oak door while the weight of her words and the looming threat settled around me like an oppressive cloak. My mind raced with the potential dangers and the stark reality that, once again, my peaceful retirement was about to be disrupted in ways I hadn't anticipated.

"Uhhh, Howie?" Sammy said, making me jump about a foot in the air.

"What?" I responded. How did Sammy get in here?

"I heard everything," he said, his voice projecting from across the room.

Oh! I quickly made my way to the end table, where I had left my phone, when the doorbell rang. I forgot Sammy was on the other line when I answered Jack's call! What a morning this had been already.

"Sammy! Hey! Sorry about that," I told him.

"I heard your conversation with Detective Rodriguez, but I'm having a hard time believing it. Were the fires really arson? And what is this about someone threatening you? And they're canceling the festival? What the heck is going on? Everything was fine last night when we were working on the floats. Now it's all upside down."

"Yep. She showed me a threatening note the arsonist left at the scene. Here, let me send you the picture."

Upon seeing the picture I took of the note, I paused, my fingers hesitating over the send button. A ball of anxiety tightened in my stomach at the sight of the harsh, jagged letters glaring back at me, offering a stark reminder of the danger to our seemingly peaceful town.

"Wow, this is really bad, man," Sammy said after seeing the picture. "What are you going to do about it?"

"What am *I* going to do about it? Have you forgotten I'm retired? The Boulder Police Department is more than capable of handling this."

"But I heard the detective say she wants you to look at some old case files," Sammy reminded me.

Ever since Detective Rodriguez arrested Sammy for murder last Christmas, their relationship was strained. However, I noticed for the moment he only seemed concerned with finding out who did this.

"Yes." I nodded. "I'll review the files, but other than that, my days of chasing bad guys are behind me."

"I heard you mention that one guy to Detective Rodriguez," Sammy started.

"Derrick Harland," I reminded him.

"Yeah, him! Whatever happened to him?"

"He skipped town. Completely in the wind. But not before threatening me."

"Refresh my memory; why didn't you arrest him again?" Sammy asked.

I pinched the bridge of my nose, sighing at the ugly memory. "Couldn't. Not enough evidence. There are several others, of course, but he's just the first one who came to mind. But it has been so long since some of these incidents. It's hard to say. There's an activist who has tried to get the festival canceled every year too."

"Why?"

"She claimed it hurt the environment and was wasteful."

"She sounds like a good possibility."

As Sammy and I continued to discuss the possibilities, I crossed the room to retrieve my cup of half-forgotten coffee cooling on the counter. The old wooden floorboards creaked softly under my feet.

There was a pause on the other end, and I could almost see Sammy's knowing grin through the phone. His soft chuckle confirmed my assumption. Yes, I get it; last Christmas, when I also swore I was too old for this work, I ended up neck-deep in an investigation to get my friend out of jail.

"Howie, since when do you sit anything out? I recall you diving into more than a few messes," he paused, loudly clearing his throat to make a point, "because it was the *right* thing to do, not because it was easy."

I leaned against the kitchen counter and stared out the window at the quiet street. "I'm not the young man I used to be. Have you forgotten the danger I faced trying to clear your name last Christmas?"

"Age may have slowed your body down, but it hasn't slowed down your brain," Sammy retorted. "Hey, remember that warehouse drug bust? You figured out it was a front two days before anyone else. And don't get me started on that bank fraud case."

I groaned softly, rubbing a hand along my face. "Yeah, but that was then. What if I'm not up to it anymore? What if I don't *want* to be up to it? This was supposed to be my time to take it easy. Me and Scooby have a lot of fishing to do after all." At that, Scooby looked up with a gentle bark from his spot in the window where he was no doubt hoping for more visitors.

Sammy's voice softened. "Listen, old friend, fear of stepping back into this life is normal, I'm sure. But I've seen you in action; heck, I've seen you think circles around rookies half your age. There's still plenty of fight left in you, Detective. I'm a personal testament to that."

I inhaled deeply, feeling the weight of his words. In the meantime, Scooby padded over to sit beside me, his warm presence a silent reassurance. I scratched behind his ears while his tail thumped softly against the cabinets.

"You might be right, Sammy. Maybe it's not about being *able* to do it, but whether I *should*. This is personal. And if there's a chance to stop it before it worsens..."

"That's the Howie I know," Sammy said, a smile in his voice. "You didn't so much choose the quiet life, my friend. It just borrowed you for a while. Even if it's just for one more round. Promise me you'll at least consider it."

I nodded, more to myself than to him. "Okay. I guess I can at least do that."

"That's the spirit! I'll let you get back to your sleuthing, but call me if you need anything. I'll help in any way I can."

"Thanks," I told him before ending the call. An odd mixture of dread and determination stirred within me. As if reading my mind as he often does, Scooby nudged my hand with his nose to encourage me. A smile pulled on the corners of my mouth. "Looks like our fishing expedition will have to wait a bit, Scoobs."

Chapter 4

I finished my now cold oatmeal. The final bites mingled with thoughts of the day ahead. Scooby stared at me, his soulful brown eyes fixed on every spoonful. I offered him a blueberry, which I'm convinced he laughed about before spitting it out. "I feel you, boy, but they're good for us," I explained.

Scooby obviously didn't care, returning to his perch in the window where the sun came in full strength, and he rolled onto his back, enjoying the warmth on his belly. In the distance, someone fired up their lawn mower, and I almost envied their ignorance. So far, Boulderites were unaware the city could be under siege. I kind of wish *I* weren't so aware.

Some days, I wished I could carry on like a typical retiree, puttering around the house, fixing odds and ends, and yelling at kids to get off my lawn. However, as Ellie often reminded me, I'd be bored out of my mind by the afternoon. I'd like to try it sometime, though, just for kicks.

My quick shower wrapped steam across the bathroom mirror in a foggy embrace. I wiped it clear, and met my owngaze. Why was it still so surprising when a 67-year-old man stared back at me? Sure, the stiff knees often reminded me of my age, but in my head, I was still a young man. Or at least younger than 67. Yet there was a determination in my gaze that I hadn't seen in a while. Determination mixed with a hint of uncertainty.

After I dressed in my retirement uniform, as Ellie called it: jeans and a comfortable T-shirt in the summer and corduroys and a plaid flannel shirt in the winter, I asked Scooby if he wanted to go for a walk. Of course, he did. He was always up for a stroll and adventure.

After clipping the leash to his collar, we stepped outside. A passing jogger waved at us while Scooby barked a return greeting. The morning air was still relatively crisp and invigorating, smelling faintly of the neighbor's hydrangeas. That crisp morning air, however, would soon give way to the dry summer heat.

We headed where I always went when I needed advice. Lisa's grave. When she was alive, she was my sounding board for every puzzling case that crossed my desk. We'd sit on the creaky porch swing, coffee in hand or maybe a beer, depending on the time of day, as I laid out facts and theories that popped into my head. She'd listen intently. Her insightful questions and gentle suggestions often guided me to the answers, many of which were hidden in plain sight all along. I missed her every moment of every day.

The walk to Lisa's grave was quiet for a Saturday morning; the only sounds were our footsteps and the occasional hello from passing neighbors. As people woke up and learned about the fire, they would surely wonder how something like that could happen. Thankfully, they didn't yet know what I knew. Let them enjoy their calm before the storm. Maybe we could catch the arsonist quickly, and they'd never know the difference. They'd never know that an evil person lurked within our midst and the festival was nearly canceled.

The cemetery was a short walk from our home. Nestled on a gentle slope, it offered a perfect view of the Boulder Flatirons, standing guard over all who rested here. Scooby and I followed the winding path to Lisa's grave.

Her final resting place lay under the shade of a young aspen, its leaves whispering in the gentle breeze. The surrounding headstones were neatly arranged—many decorated in red, white, and blue for the holiday. It's so peaceful here. Even Scooby knew to be respectful.

I sighed while reaching for Lisa's headstone. The marble was cool and smooth under my touch, and the inscription read 'Beloved wife, mother, and friend.' A testament to the woman I had loved. I planted snapdragons in a colorful pot last week, and I was pleased to see they were bloom- ing already. Their pink and yellow flowers provided a stark contrast tothe gray stone and made me smile. I felt Lisa's presence in this sacred space, a comforting reminder that although the world kept turning, some bonds remained unbroken.

I knelt beside her grave, tracing the letters etched in the cool marble. Scooby, ever my shadow, settled quietly near- by, his eyes occasionally scanning the serene landscape.

"Lis, honey, you wouldn't believe the morning I've had. An arsonist destroyed some of the 4th of July floats. They were just about ready, too." I paused, the truth of the words sinking in. "And there was a note..." I hesitated again as if she were right there with me, but I didn't want to ruin her day by telling her someone threatened me. Even then, when I told her about the note, I could scarcely believe it. Someone from my past had already committed arson and was threatening the festival. Who would do such a thing?

I shifted my stance to get more comfortable by taking a seat next to the headstone while I picked at a blade of grass nearby. "I'm not sure what to make of it or who would go through all this trouble to taunt me. Me! Can you believe it? It's been years since I've been involved directly in any case, let alone something like this. But whoever did this, they know enough about me to push the right buttons."

My hand drifted to my chin, rubbing it thoughtfully. "And there's Laura Rodriguez, the detective on the case. I told you about her last Christmas. She thinks I could help, given my history with these things. But stepping back into that world? I'm not sure I'm ready for it or even if it's the right thing to do."

I paused, while the cemetery remained quiet except for a gentle breeze rustling through the trees. "You won't like this," I told her as if she were sitting in front of me and would be mad at what I was about to share. "Detective Rodriguez said if we don't catch the arsonist, they'll cancel the festival."

Lisa loved the festival. 4th of July was one of her favorite holidays, and she always served on the event committee. Shealso entered the jam-making contest every summer. She even won first place a couple of times. Her rhubarb blueberry preserves were out of this world.

"If I don't do something, if I just sit back, what happens next? What if someone gets hurt?" My voice caught slightly, a mix of frustration and resolve. "I know what you'd say: 'H. Doing the right thing is never the wrong thing.'"

Sitting back on my heels, I sighed deeply, the early morning's events on a constant loop in my mind. "I guess

I've got some thinking to do, huh? Maybe a bit of that old detective spark is still in me after all. I don't like to admit this, but when I worked on Sammy's case last Christmas, I kind of enjoyed it. But oh, how I wish you were here to talk this through with me." I let my hand linger against the cool, smooth stone for a moment longer before I stood up; Scooby immediately stood with me, ready to follow wherever I led.

As we started to leave the area, Scooby stopped in his tracks, staring at something in a nearby tree. "What is it, boy?" I followed his line of sight to a red chickadee flitting in and out of the tree branches, picking at the bark, just busy, busy, busy. Scooby and I paused, transfixed at the sight of the tiny bird when it dawned on me. I knew who the arsonist was.

Chapter 5

Scooby and I headed back home, our pace quickened by the urgency of my discovery. We climbed the stairs to the Tudor-style house I shared with Lisa for many decades. After she passed several years ago, family and friends were certain I'd sell it and buy a condo in Boca, where I'd spend my years fishing, golfing, and discussing the early bird menu at Lucille's BBQ. Admittedly, there were days when that sounded appealing, but I wasn't quite ready for that.

Our home stood proudly on a well-kept lot, its distinctive half-timbered facade and steeply pitched gable roof cast an elegant silhouette against the summer sky. The large, leaded glass windows gleamed in the late June sun, throwing light patterns across the wrap-around porch where Scooby and I often sat watching the world go by. The landscaping was in full bloom, with lush hydrangeas and towering foxgloves adding bursts of color, while neatly trimmed hedges framed the property with a sense of order and tradition - just as I liked it.

Once we got inside, I unhooked the leash, carefully placing it on the coat rack next to the door. I preferred to keep things tidy and organized—a throwback to my days in the army. The neat house kept my mind tidy as well. Scooby ran to his water bowl for a long drink. When we left, it was still cool like most summer mornings in Colorado, but it rapidly gave way to the dry summer heat, and he was parched.

I climbed the creaky wooden stairs to the attic, where I stored notes from many of my old cases in a locked file cabinet. The attic was filled with the faint scent of aged wood and memories tucked away in cardboard boxes and old trunks. Shafts of light streamed through several small, cobwebbed windows over which I scolded myself for failing to keep them dusted. In the corner, my battered yet sturdy metal file cabinet stood guard; its faded green paint, chipped and rusted in spots, held decades of old case files stacked neatly in its deep, squeaky drawers.

The little red bird in the cemetery reminded me of one of my first cases, and I needed to double-check my notes to refresh my memory. Sliding open the long, heavy drawer, I thumbed through the file folders until I found it—the file on Marcus Parot, who pronounced his name like 'parrot', despite the spelling, and who often referred to himself as 'The Bird.'

He was a local handyman known for his quick temper and erratic behavior. Before his arrest, he had a small handyman business that struggled financially, often leading to conflicts with clients and other local businesses. He felt marginalized and blamed others for his misfortunes, cultivating a growing resentment towards those he saw as more successful or influential.

After months of investigations, we finally nailed Marcus for a pair of revenge fires at a local restaurant that had terminated their contracts with him. Despite being a newly minted detective, I linked the fires to Marcus through forensic evidence and surveillance footage, with a bit of dumb luck thrown in for measure when we caught Marcus purchasing large quantities of lighter fluid. (Have I mentioned the best part about most criminals was that they're dumb?)

The jury returned a guilty verdict as we knew they would. It was a slam dunk case. But Parot's frustration and anger boiled over once the jury read the verdict. In a courtroom packed with media, victims, and law enforcement, he leaped to his feet and attempted to jump the barrier before shouting at me, "I'm warning you! You'll pay for this, O'Sullivan! You can't keep me down forever!"

I double-checked my old notes to make sure I didn't mistake how it went down. Nope. There it was in my ownhandwriting - a historical account of my experience with Marcus Parot.

But the most important part, if I remembered it correctly, was his release date. Yes, there it was—one week ago—just in time to make good on his threats. I re-read a copy of the note he sent me shortly after he went to prison.

They can't keep me locked up forever, and someday, when you least expect it, O'Sullivan, your luck will run out, and I'll be back with an explosive surprise.

I compared that note to the one left at the crime scene today:

This is only the beginning. Cancel the 4th of July Festival, or the fireworks won't be the only explosion in town. You got lucky last time, O'Sullivan. It won't happen again.

Check and check. These notes had to have been written by the same person. Unfortunately, I couldn't compare handwriting because the note he sent me from prison was written on a typewriter. But the message was clearly the same. Adding to the intrigue, the note Parot sent me from prison was never made public, so the only people who would know about this, aside from the police department, were me and Marcus Parot. Reviewing the file convinced me he was our guy, or it at least put him at the top of the suspect list.

"Hey, Scooby! Wanta go for a ride?" I don't know why I even asked. Of course, he wanted to go for a ride. I'd know something was wrong if he turned down a truck ride. Scooby raced to the door leading to the garage, eager for me to move at the same pace. After I opened the passenger door, he waited for me to scoop him up because our veterinarian often warned me to be mindful of his long back. I carefully placed him in his canine car seat, buckling him in as he licked my face in gratitude. What a silly dog. After Lisa passed, I adopted him from the Humane Society of Boulder Valley because Ellie insisted I needed a companion.

I wasn't sure at first that I wanted the responsibility of caring for a dog, and I hadn't a clue about dachshunds, but now I'm almost embarrassed to admit that Scooby was exactly what I needed, and I can't believe I ever doubted it. Who doesn't need unconditional love, boundless enthusiasm, and loyal companionship? He has enriched my life with joy, comfort, and laughter, and he always seemed to know when I needed it most.

I settled myself in the driver's seat and opened the garage door. After an unfortunate incident last Christmas, I had to buy a new truck for the first time in 30 years, which I'm still bitter about. Forget almost dying. I loved that truck. Who cares if the heater only worked sporadically? It was a steadfast and loyal pickup.

But Ellie eventually talked me into a cherry red Ford F-150. She reasoned that I hadn't bought a new truck in 30 years, and I had to consider all the money I'd saved, so I should splurge on this one. I resented the new pickup at first. At times, I still thought it was ridiculous. But I admit it was nice to have a working heater. And this one even had heated seats! And a heated steering wheel! I didn't realize those even existed. I was certain I'd never use all the gizmos it came with, but I secretly appreciated some of the upgrades. If I'm driving and Ellie texts me, the truck reads it to me and even lets me respond without taking my eyes off the road. It's a far cry from a truck that still had a cassette player.

As I drove to the police station, I was poignantly reminded of Boulder's tranquil beauty and how, no matter where I went, the scenery was breathtaking. It infuriated me someone was out there threatening to disturb that. Unaware of the possible lurking danger, Boulderites jogged along tree-lined paths and sipped coffee outside quaint cafés, enjoying the serenity of our fantastic town. The stark contrast between the town's peaceful exterior and the hidden menace of a madman on the loose weighed heavily on me.

With each mile, I gripped the steering wheel tighter as my protectiveness for this beautiful city and its people kicked in. By the time we pulled into the police station parking lot, I was more convinced than ever that Marcus Parot was behind this, and I was certain that the moment Detective Rodriguez saw the file and heard what I had to say, she would undoubtedly dispatch a patrol car to pick him up, and this would all be over soon.

It still felt odd to park in guest parking at the police station and not behind the locked gates like I used to. The exterior of the Boulder police station was made of a sturdy, deep red brick, while the entrance was framed by broad, clear glass doors bordered by panels of the same red brick. Above the doors, a modest sign bore the city's emblem and the words "Boulder Police Department" in simple, bold letters against a brushed metal background.

The meticulously maintained landscaping reminded me I needed to mow my own lawn and pull some weeds that threatened to take over. Low-growing shrubs and hardy, drought-resistant grasses lined the walkway, with several ancient maple trees planted at strategic points, providing much-needed shade.

Off to one side, a small, well-kept memorial garden dedicated to fallen officers offered a spot of solemnity and reflection. Benches faced a delicately carved stone memorial surrounded by clusters of purple coneflowers and wild lupines, adding a splash of color and a sense of peace to the setting.

As I pushed open the station's solid glass doors, a wave of nostalgia hit me. The familiar scent of industrial-strength cleaner mixed with the faint trace of coffee felt like home. The lobby hadn't changed much; it still had the same utilitarian tile floors that echoed every footstep, along with the outdated beige walls and fluorescent lights that cast a dull glow over everything.

The low buzz of conversation, punctuated by the sporadic crackle of radio static and the clack of keyboards, surrounded me. I checked in at the front desk and got a visitor badge, which was always a mere formality given my many, many years on the job.

Getting back to Detective Rodriguez' desk was a challenge because of all the chitchatting Scooby and I inevitably did with all my old friends. Still, eventually we located the good detective who was hard at work behind her cluttered desk, her brow wrinkling as she shuffled through piles of paperwork and ignored her constantly ringing phone.

"Detective." She nodded at me with an amused expression. "Scooby," she added, smiling at my dog, who barked and wiggled his tail furiously, always hoping there was a treat hidden in her pocket. "Your text message intrigued me," she said.

"I figured it would," I told her, holding out the case file. "What Marcus Parot said when I helped put him away and the note today were far too similar."

When she opened the file on her desk, I tapped on the note, much like she did this morning at my house.

She nodded. "You're right. They are really similar. But I don't know that it guarantees he's our guy."

"But note his release date. The timing is awfully convenient for someone who once vowed to get back at me."

"It's suspicious enough that I think we should look into it. I know his parole officer, Gavin Colle. I'll call him."

"Great. So my job here is done." I turned on my heel, ready to hurry from the precinct and back home to mow my lawn. But before I could leave, a man stuck his head around the corner.

"Detective!" he shouted at her. "You have a call on line three you have to take."

"Now?"

"Yes. Now. It's urgent."

"Hang on a second, O'Sullivan, and I'll walk out with you," Rodriguez said. "I wanted to chat with you about the additional names you texted me earlier."

"Of course."

"Detective Rodriguez here," she said into the phone. "What? When? We'll be right there," she responded, glancing up at me with a concerned expression.

We? Surely, she can't be talking about me. Why was she looking at me like that? I had a sinking feeling something had gone very wrong. But before I could ask, my phone buzzed with a text.

Gramps. I've been in an accident. Can you come get me? P.S. I'm okay.

Chapter 6

As an Army veteran and retired detective, I don't rattle easily. Not even close. I will admit, however, that a text from my granddaughter telling me she's been in an accident nearly sent me over the edge. But as I prepared to bolt from the station, Detective Rodriguez hung up the phone, and we exclaimed in stereo, "Ellie was in an accident!"

"Wait. How did you know?" I asked, dumbfounded.

"That was the highway patrol. C'mon, I'll drive you," she said in a surprisingly calm fashion.

"Is it oka--" I nodded at Scooby, but Rodriguez cut me off before I finished.

"You really have to ask?"

We scrambled from the station, papers scattering in our wake, officers quickly stepping aside before we shoved through the front door. Thirty seconds ago, I planned to go home and mow the lawn. Now, my world teetered on collapse.

As I followed Detective Rodriguez to her cruiser, my legs propelled me forward with a strange mix of adrenaline and dread. Scooby and his stubby dachshund legs scrambled to keep up. We got in, and I clicked the seatbelt as my thoughts raced uncontrollably—images of Ellie, hurt and alone, flashed before my eyes, tightening the knot of panic in my stomach. As the cruiser engine roared to life and the siren wailed, a cold sweat broke across my forehead

Detective Rodriguez maneuvered the cruiser through traffic with practiced urgency, the siren announcing a desperate plea to the world around us. I know Ellie said she was okay, but it's hard to predict how accurate that was. She got that from me. What does *okay* mean? I know I could have a concussion and stitches, but still insist I was okay. Was it more serious than she let on? The adrenaline she undoubtedly experienced at the moment could mask any real injuries. What if she had a traumatic brain injury? Or internal bleeding? I'm supposed to look out for her. Her mother would be furious. Oh no. Her mother. I wonder if she knew. Should I tell her? Should I wait until I know more? My mind was awhirl with near panic.

"How bad do you think it is, Laura?" I finally managed to ask, my voice rough, the words barely squeezing past the lump in my throat. "Even though Ellie said she's okay, she could be covering up something serious to keep me from panicking."

The detective's eyes were fixed on the road, her hands steady on the wheel, navigating the blur of passing cars with a grim determination while she shook her head. "Accident Investigation said it was serious, but they didn't give me details. Just that it was Ellie, of course," she replied, her voice firm but not without empathy. She knew Ellie was not just my granddaughter but a part of my heart.

"What aren't you telling me?" I asked sharply. There was something about the way she was talking that made me suspicious.

She groaned. "You'll find out eventually, so I might as well tell you now. The investigators at the scene say a witness swore the SUV that ran her off the road did it on purpose."

"No way." Surely, they're mistaken. *I* was purposely run off the road last Christmas. I insisted it was impossible at the time, but I was wrong. Now, they're saying my granddaughter was run off the road? What if it's Parot? I swear if he tried to harm Ellie...

Rodriguez threw me a sharp glance, her focus shifting momentarily from the road. "Don't go there, Detective. We don't have any evidence that it's related to the case. Accidents happen, and that's all we know right now."

"But what if it wasn't an accident? What if Parot, or whoever destroyed the floats and threatened me, is using Ellie to get at me?"

"We'll figure it out. Right now, let's just go to the scene and make sure she's okay. Focus on that," she said, her tone softening, trying to anchor me back to reality from the tormenting sea of 'what ifs.'

As we rounded the corner and the accident scene came into view, my heart lodged firmly in my throat, and for a moment, the world stopped. The sight of flashing red and blue lights and Ellie—my vibrant, fearless granddaughter—was perched on the back end of an ambulance, with a paramedic gently tending to her. Or at least trying to. Ellie didn't appear to be cooperating—another family trait. Scooby, who I held firmly on my lap, whined and barked when he spotted Ellie. Detective Rodriguez barely stopped the car when I leaped from the door, but hesitated when I realized I was still holding Scooby.

"I'll take him; go see her," Detective Rodriguez insisted, reaching out her arms. Thankfully, Scooby was happy to be handed over to her. He tried to lick her face, and she laughed.

I ran for Ellie, and as I approached, she looked up. Her face was pale, and her smile was forced for my sake, trying to reassure me before I even reached her.

"Gramps," she called out softly. I couldn't speak; I only reached out and enveloped her in a firm embrace while the paramedic stepped back to give us a moment.

"What happened?" I asked, trying to keep my voice steady, but the edges were frayed with concern.

She nodded, brushing her blonde bangs from her light blue eyes, revealing a small butterfly bandage on her forehead. My heart clenched painfully at the vivid and unsettling reminder of the danger that had brushed so perilously close to my beloved granddaughter.

"I was driving to the bookstore for my shift, and this black SUV started tailgating me big time. At first, I thought maybe they were just in a hurry, but then they didn't pass. They just kept getting closer." Her hands fidgeted with the hem of her shirt, a nervous habit she had since she was a little girl.

"And then what happened?" I urged gently, keeping my tone soft.

She took a deep breath, steadying herself. "It got really scary, Gramps. They started swerving towards me like they were trying to hit me. I tried to speed up, to get away, but they matched every move. Then, they bumped me. It was so sudden, I... I lost control a little and ended up there," she gestured to the side of the road, her voice quivering.

A cold shiver crawled down my back, and my fists tightened instinctively. "Did you see who was driving? Could you tell anything about them?"

She shook her head, frustration and fear mingling in her eyes. "No, the windows were tinted super dark. I couldn't see inside at all. It was just so fast."

She pointed to her car perched sideways in what thankfully appeared to be a shallow ditch at the side of the road. The tow truck was pulling it out as we watched. Not that I cared that much about the car, but I didn't think her green Subaru sustained too much damage.

Putting my arm around her shoulders, I pulled her in, needing to reassure both her and myself. "You did good, Ellie. You're safe; that's what matters." I paused, looking into her eyes, making sure she understood my next words. "Detective Rodriguez reported that a witness said it looked like they did it on purpose. I'm concerned someone targeted you—because of me."

"The witness is still here," she said, pointing to a man talking to the traffic investigators. She appeared confused about my assertion, and I realized she didn't know about the arson or threat against me, which I would have to explain later. But right now, I needed to get to the witness.

But, just as I was about to approach him, Rodriguez and Scooby headed our way. Scooby desperately pulled on the leash, and the detective looked like she had trouble keeping up.

"Scoobs!" Ellie cried, throwing the blanket from her shoulders and leaning down to grab Scooby, who leaped into her waiting arms.

"I couldn't hold him back," Detective Rodriguez puffed. "He's strong for such a little guy."

I shook my head. "There's no holding a dachshund back when they want something. Excuse me, please, but I need a word with the witness," I told everyone around me.

"I'm coming with you," Rodriguez insisted.

"Don't you trust me?" I asked.

"I'm worried you're already taking this too personally."

"But it *is* personal," I reminded her.

"And that's why you need an escort," she said, pursing her mouth.

"Fine. Let's go."

Chapter 7

After talking to the witness, I returned to a waiting Ellie, where the EMT continued to monitor her despite Scooby trying to give them both kisses. I maintained a close watch, anxiously hovering nearby. She looked more frazzled than injured, but still, one couldn't be too cautious about matters like this.

"I'll ride with you in the ambulance to the hospital," I insisted, my voice cracking with concern.

Ellie shook her head firmly, her expression stubborn. "Gramps, I'm fine, really. It's just a few scrapes. Hospitals are for sick people, and I don't want to spend the rest of the day there for nothing."

"How do you know it's nothing?" I countered. "You were run off the road, Ellie. This isn't just a bump or a scrape from falling off a bike."

In typical O'Sullivan fashion, she ignored that part. "What did the witness say? And why would someone want to run *me* off the road? I'm nobody." When Detective Rodriguez and I turn to each other, our expressions somber, Ellie sits up straighter. "What? Do you really think they're trying to get to you through me? Why?"

"You obviously saw the news this morning with the floats on fire at Boulder Memorial Park," I started.

"Yes! That was horrible. What happened? It was an accident, right?"

"We don't think so," I said slowly.

"What do you mean you don't think so?"

"It looks like arson, and we have reason to believe it's revenge against me." I left out the part about the note for the time being. Too many extra ears are listening in.

Ellie gasped while the EMT standing next to her looked too interested for my taste. Why won't he just go away? "So the witness was right?" she asked. "The person in the SUV purposefully ran me off the road?"

"Yes."

"Did he get a good look at whoever it was?" she asked hopefully.

"No." I shook my head. "He said the same thing you did: that the windows were heavily tinted. However, he noticed a membership sticker from the Green Horizons League on the back window. But that's enough chit-chat," I insisted because the paramedic's interest was making me uncomfortable. "Can we get to the hospital now?"

"Gramps. I'm serious. I'm not going."

The paramedic, who was still hanging around, listening to our conversation and smiling at my granddaughter a little more than I'd like, interjected, "She's stable, sir. No signs of concussion, and her vitals are strong. If she refuses to go to the hospital, I can't make her. She should still be monitored, and rest is crucial."

I glared at him extra hard when I saw Ellie beaming up at him. Ugh. Thanks for nothing, pal. "I give up. But you're coming home with me," I insisted.

"But Gramps," she protested.

"Nope!" I held up my hand. "It's either to the hospital or to my house. That's my final offer."

"All right. I give in. I'll go home with you. For now!" she added. "But what about my car?"

"I told the tow truck driver to take it to Sid's Auto Body, where I've always gone. I trust him. But now we'll have to go back to the station for my pickup."

"If I may." Detective Rodriguez stepped in. "Officer Katz can take Ellie and Scooby back to your house. He'll stay on-site to ensure it's secure so you and I can return to the station and review the list of suspects you sent me. I promise I won't keep you too long so you can get back to taking care of your granddaughter." Detective Rodriguez smiled at Ellie.

Reluctantly, I nodded, the compromise easing a bit of my worry. "Alright, Ellie, but remember how adamant you were that I rest after *my* accident. I'm holding you to the same standard."

Ellie managed a small, reassuring smile. "If I remember correctly, you *barely* rested after your accident."

"I took a day off," I reminded her.

"Whatever. Just go catch whoever did this to me. And be safe!" she insisted.

I gave her one more tight squeeze and rubbed Scooby's head, who was still having far too much fun. As we drove back to the station, I realized I no longer had a choice. I had to help solve this. Retired or not, busting the arsonist was my first priority. Funny how a world I thought I had left behind with my retirement somehow kept pulling me back in.

"It's Parot," I said, the conviction in my voice firmer than I had intended. "You saw the notes in the file I gave you. It can't be a coincidence." Detective Rodriguez, ever the voice of reason, asked for specifics. I suspected she was trying to distract me, but I was grateful for the excuse to talk about anything other than the accident.

"Marcus always had a knack for dramatics and threats. He referred to himself as 'The Bird' and liked to think he was someone who watched over the city, viewing everything from a high vantage point. So, seeing a bird at the cemetery this morning made me think of him. It was so ordinary, yet so oddly timed, and I took it as a sign."

"What was his background like? Before you put him away," she pressed.

I slid my hands down my face, hoping to recall the tinier details. "He was a typical ne'er do well. We'd get called down to a bar where he was causing trouble. Standard drunk and disorderly type stuff. His handyman business often struggled, and he had public fights with clients. When he set the fires at a couple of small businesses that had terminated their contracts with him, he used lighter fluid to do it."

"But you suspected he was gearing up for something bigger?" Detective Rodriguez asked.

I nodded vigorously. "Absolutely. As time passed, his troubles intensified. I have to admit, though, I was a little surprised when the judge threw the book at him."

"You expected differently?"

"Kind of." I wiggled my hand back and forth. "He hadn't injured anyone yet, but I could see where it was headed."

"Earlier, you said he lost it in the courtroom?"

"Absolutely. He freaked. It took three guards to drag him out of there."

"Do you suppose this is what led the judge to impose the sentence that she did?" Rodriguez asked.

"That's a good point. I didn't even think of that. But you may want to alert her as well about Parot. Send a patrol car through her neighborhood, too."

"Will do." Rodriguez nodded. "And I agree with your assessment. Very possible he could be our guy," she surmised as we pulled into the police station parking lot.

Back at the station, an uneasy solemnity settled over me. The always familiar buzz of the precinct now came with a heightened sense of urgency. We navigated through the corridors lined with bustling officers and ringing phones, and now that I've agreed to involve myself, each step reignited old instincts. By the time we reached Rodriguez' cluttered workspace, a grim determination had taken hold. Here, amidst the familiar bustle of ongoing cases and crime reports, I felt an old part of myself awaken, ready to dive back into the fray, driven by a need to protect my family and serve my community once more.

"Ronnie, my assistant, pulled these files after you texted the names this morning," she told me, handing me a short stack of files. "Mary Beth is out on maternity leave, so you can use her desk. Look through them and let me know what jumps out at you." She pointed to an empty desk in the corner. "Meanwhile, I'll contact Parot's parole officer."

I did as Rodriguez told me, settling into the creaky desk chair and spreading the documents before me. While I could hear Rodriguez on the phone, I couldn't hear her well enough to make out the particulars of what she was saying. I was getting a lot of mmms and ahhs. I desperately wanted to hear her more clearly, but I needed to focus on these files. If I *had* to pick only one, Parot would still be my primary suspect. How could he not be? The note left at the crime scene this morning was too similar to the same threat he made against me many years ago. But like any other case, I knew everything must be investigated thoroughly. A short while later, Rodriguez hung up the phone before pulling up a chair beside me.

"I've got good news and bad news."

"When are we bringing Parot in for questioning?" was my response.

"We're not. Not at this moment anyway," she said, responding to my shocked reaction. "Just hear me out," she insisted, raising her hand to ward off my protest. "According to Parot's parole officer, he was a model prisoner."

"Oh, please. Like we haven't seen that before," I grumbled, rolling my eyes. "Doesn't make him innocent now."

"I understand that, but his parole officer swears he underwent a significant transformation in prison and has repeatedly maintained prison was the best thing that ever happened to him. He even became an ordained minister," Rodriguez added, referring to her notes. "He counseled other inmates, worked in the prison library, and once managed to negotiate a truce between an inmate and a guard during a dangerous standoff."

I flashed back to the man who threatened me in the courtroom. The man who once set revenge fires with no regard for who it could harm. Could he have genuinely turned his life around, or was it only a facade? The doubt gnawed at me, but the stakes were too high to overlook critical details. Yet it still conflicted with the gut feeling I had carried for years.

Detective Rodriguez recognized the skepticism on my face. "People can change, O'Sullivan. Maybe he found something in there to believe in, something to change his life's trajectory."

"So you don't think we should bring him in for questioning?" I pressed.

"His parole officer has agreed to talk to him for us. He feels like Parot trusts him and will open up to him. If we bring him in now and he actually is guilty, he might bolt or cover his tracks."

"Fair enough. But If I find additional evidence that points to him, I'll insist you bring him in right away."

"Agreed." She nodded. "Now, what else have you found? You didn't include details when you sent me the names of potential suspects earlier, so I'm eager to know more. Tell me about Marah Sterling," she said, nodding at the file sitting on top.

"She was an activist who studied environmental science in college, then became a professional activist after gradu-ation." As Rodriguez' eyes met mine, I paused to point to Sterling's employer, Green Horizons League.

"I suspect there are a lot of people who have that sticker on their vehicle but duly noted," she acknowledged. "Isn't she the one who has fought to get the 4th of July Festi-val canceled?"

"That's her. And for many years. As you can imagine, she's no fan of mine. She's respected in the community for her dedication to environmental causes, but she also has a darker, more radical side."

"Radical enough to commit arson?" Rodriguez asked, raising an eyebrow.

"She told a reporter last year that the town should enjoy the festival one last time because she would get it canceled next year if she had to burn everything down to do it."

"That could be a rather generic threat, though, right? I mean, people tend to say things like that without literally meaning they're willing to light something on fire."

"Absolutely." I nodded. "*But* in college, she was suspended for a semester for setting fire to a trash can in the cafeteria over their refusal to permanently carry veggie burgers on the menu," I explained, holding the document up.

"I take it she's also threatened you personally."

"Yes. At a city council meeting last year, she made an impassioned plea about why the festival should be permanently canceled. She pointed at me when they denied her request and declared, 'If you and your corrupt council don't refuse to halt this wasteful festival, don't be surprised when nature fights back.'"

"You make friends wherever you go, don't you, Detective?" She grimaced.

"I'm sure you know how it is," I replied, while she nodded in agreement.

"What about this one." She shifted to a new suspect. "Trent Baxter."

"Yes. That one was just rather sad."

"He was a firefighter?"

"*Was* being the operative term. His career was abruptly derailed when he was implicated in a jewelry theft at a house fire," I explained.

"You were the lead investigator on the case?"

"I was."

"Why do you say it was sad?" Detective Rodriguez leaned forward, eager to hear more.

"Because I determined that he *didn't* steal the jewelry. And it wasn't just a lack of evidence. At the time, I didn't believe he did it, and I still don't."

"One hundred percent?" Rodriguez asked.

"One hundred percent. No doubt in my mind," I confirmed. "He was simply in the wrong place at the wrong time."

"Yet they still fired him."

"And, naturally, he felt betrayed by the system he had served so loyally. Unfortunately, he didn't handle it well, to say the least. After he got fired, he took on a series of odd jobs while facing a diminishing circle of friends due to his erratic behavior. His financial situation deteriorated, undoubtedly adding to his frustration and desperation. I heard his wife left him, too. She said she couldn't take his drinking and his temper anymore."

"So if you were the lead investigator who exonerated him, why would he blame you?"

"He felt that it was my job to publicly champion his innocence and demand the fire department reinstate him."

"But that's not your job," Rodriguez pointed out.

"Right. Besides, I think he vastly overestimated any sway I would have with the public or the fire department."

"I doubt the police department would support such tactics either," Rodriguez pointed out as I nodded in agreement.

"I assume the reason you pulled this file is that he also threatened you."

"One night at the Veteran's Hearth Bar, he had too much to drink and blamed me for his downfall. He got so belligerent that Sammy had to throw him out."

"What else makes you think he should be a suspect in this?"

"First, he was a firefighter, so he'd know more than the average person about how and where to set it and how to control it, after all, you pointed out that the fire investigation thought it was a professional job."

"What else?" she asked.

"That night at the bar, he kept saying, 'you think you're so lucky' and 'your luck will run out someday, guaranteed'!"

"So, also similar to the language in the note left at the scene."

"Close enough that it gives me pause."

"Now, what about the man you first mentioned this morning? Derrick Harland?"

"I'd consider him a career arsonist. He liked setting fires because he got a thrill from it."

Similar to Parot, I encountered Harland early in my investigative career when we suspected him of being involved in a series of arson cases. We brought him in for questioning multiple times, but he was one slippery dude who I couldn't quite pin with any of the fires. He would taunt us during interrogations, which only fueled my dislike of him and made me determined to prove he'd done it. The tension between us reached a peak when he openly threatened me during an interrogation, saying he knew where I lived and who my family was."

"Do you think he really knew? Or was he only trying to scare you?"

"He was crafty, so unfortunately, he probably knew about my family. But shortly after that incident, he was in the wind. Disappeared into thin air. No trace, no nothing. We spent years trying to find him, but nothing. I've often wondered if he met with foul play. Finally crossed the wrong person, you know? But it's just a guess. It has been a long time since I checked the crime database to see if anyone matching his description was picked up in another state."

"Okay. We'll check into these further, and I'll let you know what we find. Why don't you get home to Ellie now?"

"Will do. Thanks! Call me with any questions."

After picking up pizza from Pizzazzle's on the way home at Ellie's request, I pulled into the garage, eager to see that she and Scooby were doing as well as she claimed when the truck's dashboard dinged with a text from a blocked sender.

You're out of luck.

Chapter 8

As I stepped into my house, I was all too aware that the familiar comfort it typically offered was over-shadowed by the cryptic text message: "You're out of luck." My eyes scanned the shadows in the corners of the entry-way, half-expecting to find a threat lurking. When Scooby barreled around the corner at me, barking joyously at my arrival, I nearly jumped a foot from nerves.

"Scooby! Calm down! I told you he'd be home soon," Ellie scolded half-heartedly. We could never really be ir-ritated with Scooby, after all. "Hey, Gramps, I already set the table... uhhh, where's dinner?" she asked, noticing my empty hands. "Oh no! What's wrong?" she exclaimed when she saw my pale face.

"Huh? Oh. Yeah. I left it in the truck," I mumbled.

"Gramps. What happened?" she persisted, tugging on my elbow.

"I'll fill you in; just let me get dinner. You need to eat," I said

Back in the garage, I glanced at my phone, hoping I had imagined the text. Nope. It was still there. Despite wanting to believe it was nothing, I forwarded it to Detective Rodriguez for her opinion.

As I returned to the house, this time with pizzas in hand, I was surprised by the rich, comforting aroma of baking brownies that I hadn't noticed before.

"You promised you'd take it easy!" I chastised Ellie, who was standing in the kitchen by the stove

She shrugged. "I got bored. I'm an O'Sullivan, after all. Now spill. You look like you've seen a ghost, *and* you forgot the food in the garage. That's not like you at all."

"The brownies smell fabulous. Any trouble while I was gone?" I asked while crossing the living room to peek out the window to make sure Officer Katz was still there, even though I only saw him moments ago.

Ellie pursed her lips and planted her hands on her waist. She wouldn't let up until I admitted what was bothering me.

"Okay, okay, I got a text from a blocked number just as I was pulling into the garage," I told her, holding out the phone for her to see. "Did anything out of the ordinary happen while I was gone? Any unusual noises? You must pay attention to everything right now. Anything could be a clue," I told her.

"Nope. It was quiet as can be."

"Do you need me to take you to your apartment so we can pack a suitcase?"

"How long do you think I'll be here?" she asked, half amused and half worried even though she was trying to cover it.

"Until we catch whoever set the floats on fire and ran you off the road."

"Okay, well, I still have some things in the guest bedroom, so we're good for tonight. Gramps, how many pizzas do you plan to eat?" Ellie asked, pointing at the multiple pizza boxes.

"Jack and Sammy will be here soon," I explained.

"How many nights a week do you eat pizza?" she asked, one eyebrow raised.

"Not that many." I shrugged. "I'll wash up--" I started to say when we heard a commotion at the front door. "Stay here!" I barked at Ellie. My heart skipped a beat or two, sending a surge of adrenaline coursing through my veins. My body tensed, ready to spring into action, muscles coiled tight as my instincts to protect my family and my home kicked in. My mind raced with possibilities, each scenario playing out in rapid succession, as I quickly approached the door, forcing myself to steady my breathing against the pounding in my chest.

I reached for my gun out of instinct like I did 20 years ago when I came home after a shift. Only it's not 20 years ago, and I'm retired and no longer carry my gun on my hip. Where was Officer Katz, and what was happening at my front door? All the threats I reviewed in the files this afternoon and the recent text churned in my head. I peered out through the peephole.

"Oh, for--!" I exclaimed, throwing open the door to find a four-way staredown between Officer Katz, Sammy, Jack, and Jack's service dog, Chance. "I apologize, Officer Katz. I neglected to warn you they were coming. These are my friends Sammy and Jack. They're here for dinner."

"Oh. Sorry about that, fellas," Officer Katz said.

"I'll fix a plate for your dinner," I told him.

"Well..."

"Don't worry about it. Believe me, I remember how it is."

"Thanks," he responded somewhat sheepishly.

Sammy marched through the door, muttering while Jack and Chance followed.

"Ellie, could you put some pizza on a plate for Officer Katz and throw in some napkins and a pop while you're at it."

"You want me to take it out?" she asked.

"No!" we all exclaimed in unison.

"Sheesh. All right. I'll let you do it," Ellie grumbled.

After I took dinner to Officer Katz, Ellie, Jack, Sammy, and I settled in around the kitchen table. Scooby reluctantly let Chance share one of his beds. He was a large, eager Golden Retriever mix who was spotted by a trainer at an animal shelter in Texas. His previous owners surrendered him because he was tearing apart their house while they were at work. It turned out Chance just needed proper training and a job.

His energy made him a perfect candidate for assisting Jack. The family who trained him named him Chance because they hoped it would help him get a second chance. Scooby wasn't sure what to think when we introduced the two. He was used to being the top dog—heck, he was used to being the *only* dog. But eventually, he and Chance called a truce, and now they're friends who only squabble occasionally.

As we gathered around the table, passing out plates, pizza, napkins, and beer for just a moment, I let myself forget what was happening outside these walls. Sometimes, I wished I had more family here in Colorado, but as I looked around the table, I realized I had all the family I needed right here.

"How are you feeling?" Sammy asked Ellie as we dug into the hot, crispy, cheese-laden pizza. I didn't understand how Ellie could complain we ate it too much. Was that really possible?

"I'm fine, really. Gramps tends to exaggerate things."

"So, catch us up, old man. What's new since we learned about the fire this morning?" Jack asked.

"Show them the text, Gramps," Ellie insisted.

"What text?" Sammy asked.

I huffed loudly. I was hoping to wait until after we ate, but I reluctantly held the phone up for them.

"And you don't know who sent it?"

"Nope."

"How did everything go at the police station?" Ellie asked.

"Detective Rodriguez and I discussed what I think are the four likeliest suspects."

"You mentioned Derrick Harland this morning," Sammy said. "Could he have sent you that text? What if he's back? That dude was seriously bad news."

"Who's Derrick?" Jack asked.

"Dad was a drunk who pounded on him and his mom all the time. It was one of those homes the police were sent to on a regular basis, but then mom refused to press charges. Mom eventually died of an overdose, dad disappeared, and then Derrick was in and out of foster care, group homes, and eventually juvie. At first, it was just minor incidents like spray painting city-owned buildings and the like, but then he developed a particular fascination with fire, and as he got older, his fascination got more destructive and his behavior more erratic. I didn't meet him until he was an adult. We brought him in for questioning multiple times, but he was slippery. His taunting demeanor during interrogations only fueled my determination to prove his guilt. But then he disappeared."

"So he definitely could have sent you that text. From what you're saying, it sounds like something he would do," Jack pointed out.

"Yes, him or a man named Marcus Parot. However, Detective Rodriguez checked with his parole officer. He claims Parot was a model prisoner, became a pastor, and counseled other prisoners. Supposedly, he even stopped a prison riot once."

"You don't believe it?" Sammy said.

I shrugged. "Convicts aren't always known for telling the truth. It could be a long con that he's playing. His parole officer will talk to him. Find out where he was when the float fires started."

"Who's the other suspect, Gramps?"

"An activist named Marah Sterling."

"Oh! I know her!" Ellie exclaimed.

"You do?" I asked in surprise.

"Well, I know *of* her. She's always on campus giving lectures and meeting with student leaders about becoming activists. Do you really think she could have set the fires?"

"She's been trying to get the 4th of July Festival shut down for years. Given that I'm one of the leaders, you can imagine how she feels about me. She even threatened me during a city council meeting."

"Gramps! You never told me that!"

"I didn't think much of it at the time. Do you know how many enemies I made as a cop? People threatened to do stuff to me on a regular basis."

"You said there were four suspects you think needed investigating?" Jack asked.

"Yeah. There's also a disgruntled former firefighter who was accused of stealing jewelry from a home where they responded to a fire."

"Oh, that's awful," Ellie remarked.

"What's especially awful is my investigation showed he was innocent, but they fired him anyway."

"That's sad he got fired anyway."

"I agree. He didn't take it well, to say the least. He harbors a deep resentment toward the fire department and the city officials he believes were responsible for his unjust firing. He often expresses his frustrations at community meetings and on social media. Because of that, he's become a person of interest in arson-related investigations in Boulder. Listen, we have to catch this arsonist for so many reasons. Not only is he--"

"--or she!" Ellie interrupted.

"--a threat to our community and my family; we can't cancel the 100th anniversary of the festival," I stressed, my eyes scanning each of their faces to gauge their understanding of the stakes. "It's a century of heritage and unity that we shouldn't take lightly. I'm concerned it would be very demoralizing for the community if it was canceled, and--"

I'm annoyed when my ringing phone interrupts my warning, but I'm concerned when I realize it's another blocked call. I put my finger against my lips to warn everyone to be quiet. "This is Howard O'Sullivan," I answer on speaker phone so they can all hear.

A distorted voice comes on the line. "Did you get my text?"

"Who is this?" I demanded.

"Ellie won't be the only one in danger if you don't cancel the festival."

Before I could respond, the call went dead.

Chapter 9

After a long, restless night, I woke early to prepare for our mission. Yes, we formulated a plan to protect the community and save the festival. Sammy, Jack, and I discussed it long into the night and determined that Parot was still our most likely suspect. How else could anyone other than him know what was in the letter he sent me so many years ago? I'm sure he was behind the text and the phone call.

Ellie went to bed early when the day's events finally got to her, which is good if you ask me. She doesn't need to be an active part of this. She agreed to stay home with Scooby today and chill. Scooby will be grateful for the company, and I felt better knowing she would stay under police protection.

No, we haven't gone rogue—not completely, anyway. I told Detective Rodriguez about the phone call right after it happened. Naturally, she was concerned, but insisted we keep an open mind regarding all the suspects and pleaded with us to tread lightly until we had more evidence.

But we didn't tell the detective about our specific plans. And once Jack realized we were serious, he plugged his ears and sang la la la like a little kid. As a lawyer, he warned us not to continue. But as our friend, he knew us too well to think we'd heed his advice.

I wasn't worried about it because I was retired and had nothing to lose. Sammy didn't care, period. But we didn't want Jack to jeopardize his law license, so we agreed he should stay out of today's plot. It's not like we plan to physically harm Parot. Unless I could prove he ran Ellie off the road. Then, all bets were off. But Jack made Sammy promise he wouldn't let me do anything that would get me arrested.

When Sammy picked me up first thing this morning, I was on edge but eager to get this behind us and back to normal.

"All set?" he asked when I opened the back door and put the cooler on the seat.

"Got it!" I patted the lid. We were staking out Parrot's halfway house this morning, so I brought water and a few snacks. If we followed him around all day, hoping to catch him sabotaging the festival or engaging in some other nefarious deed, I didn't want to miss out on something crucial because one of us had to stop for a drink. Sammy's binoculars were on the seat between us, and I dug out my old camera in case we needed photographic evidence.

We only knew where Parot's halfway house was because I overheard Detective Rodriguez mentioning it while on the phone with the parole officer. She also said he was working as a janitor at one of the churches in town.

Sammy parked three houses down from the halfway house on Mapleton Street under a huge tree with low-hanging branches, so Parot would only notice us here if he were specifically looking for us.

"Hey, check out the black SUV," Sammy said.

"I swear if he gets in the SUV, I don't care if he spots us or not. We're going after him."

"I can't tell if there's a Green Horizons League sticker on it, though. I think we should just calm down," Sammy chastized me. "We don't know which car is his until we know. For now, we watch and wait."

Sammy and I spent the next thirty minutes discussing the Broncos and their new quarterback. We pondered their chances to make the playoffs this year and decided they couldn't do much worse than they had the last several seasons. When the door to the halfway house opened, and Marcus Parot stepped onto the porch, I paused to stare. He had aged, that's for sure. Hadn't we all, but I'd recognize him anywhere. His graying hair was cropped short, revealing a strong, lined forehead, and his dark eyes still held a spark of defiance. While his build was solid, his posture had a slight stoop, hinting at the toll prison took on him.

"That's him, isn't it?" Sammy asked upon seeing the troubled expression on my face.

"It sure is," I growled.

"Look! He's getting into the SUV!" Sammy exclaimed.

My eyes narrowed as I stared at Parot approaching the SUV. My fingers were on the door handle, preparing to launch myself from Sammy's truck.

"Hang on a sec," Sammy warned, grasping my shoulder. "Never mind. False alarm," he said as Parot passed the SUV and stopped next to a dingy-looking beat-up Chevy Spark that had seen better days.

"That thing has never run another car off the road," Sammy pointed out. "I'll be amazed if it runs at all," he surmised while we watched Parot make several tries before the engine turned over.

After Parot drove away from the curb, Sammy waited a beat before pulling in behind him. "Which church did you say he worked for again?"

"Boulder United Church," I told him.

"That's what I thought. But isn't that in the opposite direction?"

"It is."

"Maybe he's just going to get gas or something," Sammy suggested.

"Wherever he's going, at least we'll know about it."

We followed Parot for several blocks when, just as the light turned red, he floored it, speeding through the intersection, leaving other drivers angry and honking their horns.

"Dangnabit, he's on to us!" Sammy shouted.

"Whatever you do, don't lose him!"

"Wasn't planning on it, boss," Sammy exclaimed as he deftly maneuvered through even more angry drivers to stay on Parot's tail. "Should we call Detective Rodriguez?" he suggested.

"And say what? Hey, we're chasing Marcus Parot through Boulder after you told us to be patient?"

"That little car moves a lot faster than I expected."

After running yet another red light, this time, a large warehouse truck cut us off.

"Go around! Go around!" I shouted at Sammy.

"I'm trying!" he shouted back. "My pickup isn't as agile as his car."

By the time Sammy got around the truck, and amazingly, we weren't killed in the process, Parot was long gone.

We drove in circles for twenty minutes, searching for the car, but no luck.

"No telling where he could have hidden that thing," I fumed, pounding on the dashboard. "I told you that guy was no good. I don't care what he pretended to be in prison."

"You should call Officer Benson at your house and warn him to be extra vigilant."

"Good idea." I called Officer Benson. "Any suspicious activity?" I asked when he answered the phone.

"No. Everything has been quiet here since I came on shift about an hour ago, sir."

"Be extra vigilant."

"Copy."

"I know you won't like this, but I'm gonna say it again. You need to let Detective Rodriguez know what we just witnessed," Sammy urged.

"Yeah, you're right," I admitted. But just as I started to press the detective's number on my phone, two Boulder Fire Department trucks raced past, full lights and sirens.

"That can't be good," I said.

"They're heading in the direction of Boulder Memorial Park. You don't think..." Sammy trailed off.

"Go!" I shouted, waving Sammy onward.

He floored the pickup, and I swore I'd be impressed if we didn't get a ticket for reckless driving after this was all done. When we arrived at the parade grounds only moments after the fire trucks did, my heart sank. The judging stand for the floats was on fire. I leaped from the pickup to stare in dismay at the sight before me.

A plume of thick, black smoke billowed into the sky, stinging my nostrils with the unmistakable scent of burning wood and plastic. The stand was engulfed in flames, crackling and popping as the fire devoured everything in its path. A mix of anger and helplessness churned in my gut as I watched yet another fixture of the festival reduced to ash. That's why Parot ran when he realized we were following him. He was heading here to start another fire.

A short distance away, Detective Rodriguez screeched to a halt in her cruiser. When she saw us, her face was a mixture of surprise and disdain.

"What are you two doing here? Or do I even want to know?"

"Marcus Parot set this fire!" I exclaimed.

Chapter 10

Before Rodriguez could question me about my claim, we were interrupted by a familiar-looking woman, "Excuse me! Excuse me!" she demanded, making her way to us amidst the growing crowd of onlookers. When she shoved a microphone in our faces, I realized why I recognized her. It was Kara Belmont, a reporter for BOYX Channel 3.

She had sharp, angular features and an air of confidence that commanded attention. She wore a bold red, sharply tailored suit and was nearly as tall as me in her heels. Her glossy jet-black hair was styled in a sleek bob that framed her face just so, enhancing her piercing hazel eyes. Basically, she looked like she belonged on TV.

"Did you just say you knew who set this fire?" she asked, trying her best to stare us down. "Does that mean it was intentional? And if so, doesn't the public have a right to know? Are we in danger here?" The moment she asked if the public had a right to know, at least a half dozen onlookers moved closer, their interest peaked.

With the microphone only inches from my face, I was about to say something I probably shouldn't, but Detective Rodriguez elbowed her way between Kara and me. "Yes, you're in danger! Do you not see the fire? Everyone move back! Officer Tyler, block off this area!"

A young officer scurried over to help corral the crowd while another one grabbed a roll of yellow caution tape from his patrol car.

"Get back, folks! Get back! Please! It's for your safety!" the officers urged.

Unfortunately, Kara continued shouting questions like, "Why hasn't the public been warned?" and "What is the police department hiding from us?" I was dismayed to see the crowd listening intently. This could get ugly quickly.

Detective Rodriguez, fearing what might come out of my mouth, attempted to steer us away from the crowd when Kara shouted, "Should the public be concerned with their safety at the 4th of July Festival?"

Oh boy. That really set them off. "Is she right? Are you hiding something from us?" an elderly man shouted at the officers.

"You can't trust anyone these days, can you?" a woman called out from nearby.

Just as I started to walk back toward the crowd to say something, Rodriguez grabbed my elbow, steering me away again.

"I promise you will be updated when we have more answers! No one is in danger at this time," she shouted back to the crowd.

"Why should we trust you?" several onlookers called out in unison.

Detective Rodriguez shook her head as she continued to steer Sammy and me away from the onlookers. "That's above my pay grade," she said when we looked at her questioningly. "It's up to the chief and the mayor to answer those questions. Now, how did you arrive at the fire scene at the same time I did? And don't..." she waggled her finger at me when I opened my mouth to tell her a story, "try to con me with, oh gee, we were just headed to get donuts when we saw the firetrucks."

She knew us too well. I glanced at Sammy, who nodded his head. "We were on a stakeout," I admitted

"Where?"

"Parot's halfway house."

"Darnit O'Sullivan! I knew you'd pull something like that. It's bad enough that I have the mayor on my back looking for updates and threatening to cancel the festival.

Now, this reporter will make things ten times worse. *And* I still have to worry about what you're up to on top of it all."

"But we need to tell you what happened. It's important."

"Go ahead," she grumbled.

"Parot came out of the house looking very suspicious."

"Suspicious, how?" she asked.

"He kept glancing over his shoulder, almost like he was checking to see if he was being followed," Sammy started.

"Exactly. He stood on the porch for several minutes, looking around nervously and fidgeting with his jacket. His whole demeanor just seemed off. We were convinced he was up to something, and obviously he was," I said, pointing at the fire, which was nearly extinguished.

"He acted like he was trying to avoid being seen," Sammy continued, but I can tell from the look on Rodriguez' face that we aren't making a good argument for our case.

"Is it possible he saw *you*?" she asked.

"I doubt it," Sammy said. "We were pretty well hidden."

"This isn't adding up. How do you jump from 'he looked nervous standing on the porch' to 'he burned down the judging stand'? What aren't you telling me?"

"After that, we followed him," I offered.

"Are you telling me he led you straight here, and you watched him set the fire?" she demanded.

"Uhhh, no."

"Then what?"

"So, we followed him, but he must have made us at some point because he ran a red light to shake us," Sammy explained.

"And I assume you stopped tailing him once he ran the red light?"

"Um..." I uttered, feeling my face go warm in the process.

"Geez, you two. I can't leave you alone for a minute. You can't tail a parolee just because you have suspicions. Do you realize how much trouble we could all be in if he files a complaint?" she said sharply, giving me her best glare.

"But you should know that he didn't go to work at the church. He drove in the opposite direction," I explained.

"So, where *did* he go?" she pressed.

"We don't know. We lost him. But that's exactly my point! We lost him for a good twenty minutes, and while we were driving around looking for him, he must have come here, set the viewing stand on fire, and bolted! You must bring him in for questioning!"

"What I need is for you two to follow the rules. What if he is guilty, but you just jeopardized the case against him?"

We both stare back at her guiltily.

"I should send you home right now, but the Fire Chief obviously wants to see me," she said, nodding toward the uniformed man who had just signaled her, "and I want to keep you right where I can see you for now, so let's go."

We made our way over to the chief, who stood by the charred remains of the judging stand, his face grim. "Detective Rodriguez," he nodded as we approached. "We found these nearby," he said, holding up two evidence bags.

Rodriguez took the bags, her eyes narrowing as she read the note aloud.

Cancel the 4th of July festival, or the next fire will make the others look like a campfire, O'Sullivan. Nature will seek revenge and this town will blow up in more ways than one if you continue to ignore me.

So, another threat containing information that few people knew of, promising more destruction unless the festival was canceled. The second bag contained another bottle of lighter fluid from Maginni's Hardware store. My gut tightened with anger and frustration.

"The handwriting matches the previous note," Rodriguez said, her voice steady but laced with tension.

The chief gestured toward the smoldering debris. "We also confirmed, as I'm sure you can tell from the smell, that this fire was started the same way as the last one—with lighter fluid."

Sammy crossed his arms, looking worried. "It's like they're taunting us, daring us to stop them."

"Hey, Chief!" a firefighter shouted, waving to him.

"If you'll excuse me, I have to go. I'll let you know if we find anything new."

"Thanks, Chief," we all told him.

"I'll get this back to the lab for processing," Rodriguez said. "Even though there were no fingerprints on the first one. In the meantime, you two go home or to the bar or wherever it is that you go when you aren't needlessly interfering with a case, and let me do my job."

"But you're bringing in Parot for questioning, right?" I asked.

"I will look into it," was all she would say.

As we made our way back to our cars, my mind was awhirl with what we should do next, the weight of the investigation pressing on me. The smell of smoke lingered in the air, a persistent reminder of how serious this was.

"You guys," I said, stopping in my tracks, using my arms to block Sammy and Rodriguez from going farther.

"Trent Baxter is here." We watched him linger at the outskirts of the crowd, his gaze fixed on the scene with an unsettling intensity. "Let's go talk to him," I said, walking quickly toward him.

But before I could take another step, Detective Rodriguez' phone chimed with a text notification. "Hold up," she said. "Oh, great. It's the mayor. He wants me in his office ASAP."

"Is it about the festival?" I asked, worried she would say yes.

"There's no doubt," she responded, her mouth set in a grim line.

When we looked up again, Trent Baxter was leaving the scene in an SUV—and it was black.

Chapter 11

As badly as I wanted to follow Trent Baxter, Detective Rodriguez made us swear we wouldn't. We agreed to behave. For now, anyway. And, as we watched her drive away, the weight of our community's beloved tradition in her hands, a wild blend of anxiety and helplessness churned inside me. There was so much at stake here: the 100th anniversary of a beloved event, the community's overall safety, and, of course, my and Ellie's personal safety were all factors we had to weigh.

"We've got to catch whoever did this," I growled at Sammy. "If the mayor cancels the festival, it will hit this town hard. Obviously, I understand the need for safety, but will everyone *else* understand if the celebration is halted?"

Sammy nodded gravely. "It means a lot to Boulder—not just because it's fun and patriotic, but it's a much-needed boost for the local economy. Everyone from food vendors to entertainers to local artists all benefit."

I hung my head. Sammy's reminder about the economic consequences was sobering, and a fresh wave of anxiety coursed through me.

"But we have to put community safety at the forefront. Who knows what else this scumbag could do if left unchecked. Someone could get severely injured or even killed!" Sammy pivoted toward me, sorrow in his eyes. "We've seen our share of trouble, haven't we? And yet we're still standing. I refuse to let this town down," he said, a catch in his voice.

"Me too, buddy. Me too," I told him, clapping him on the back as we returned to his pickup. "Let's go back to my place for now. I should check on Ellie, and we can plot our next moves."

When we arrived at my house, Sammy parked in front of the patrol car, and I nodded a greeting to the officer before heading inside. The moment we stepped through the front door, Scooby acted like he always does, like I'd been gone for weeks. His tail was a blur of motion, thumping joyously against the hardwood floor, while his enthusiastic barks filled the air right before he bounded straight for us.

His entire body wiggled with delight as he leaped up to give us both a sniff and a lick. I promise you, you're missing out if you've never experienced a joyful wiener dog.

"What's up, boy? You act like you haven't seen a soul for months. Has Ellie been on her phone instead of lavishing you with attention? Hey Ellie! We're home! She's probably in the attic," I told Sammy when we didn't get a response. "She loves to poke around up there and find old things. Ellie? Ellie?" I continued to call out, moving toward the attic so she could hear me better. "Hmm. That's odd. Maybe she has her headphones on," I explained, continuing my trek up the stairs. I hope she doesn't wear them when she's out in public. I've lectured her numerous times on situational awareness, but I never knew if she took the advice to heart. I opened the creaky door and scanned the dim space, but when I realized she wasn't there, a sinking feeling gripped me. "Ellie?" I called out anyway, knowing it was useless. A powerful wave of nervous apprehension washed over me. Where was she? She wouldn't just leave without telling me. Besides, the officer would have seen her and alerted me.

When I returned to the main level, I prayed I would find Ellie chatting with Sammy because she had been in the backyard or the garage.

"She wasn't up there?" Sammy asked, his voice concerned.

"No," I responded, opening the door to the garage. It was dark, and my truck was still there. Panic took hold. "Go get Officer Benson," I told him.

Sammy rushed out the door, while Scooby, sensing something was very wrong, followed closely on my heels.

"Scooby, what happened to Ellie?" I asked. He barked in response, but I'm not sure what he said. It wasn't the first time I desperately wished he could talk. I stuck my head out the back door, hoping she'd be in the backyard, but deep down, I knew she was gone.

While I tried not to panic further, Sammy and Officer Benson burst through the front door, their faces pale and drawn with worry. Sammy's usually steady hands trembled slightly as he ran them through his short hair while Officer Benson clenched his jaw, the tension evident in the rigid set of his shoulders.

"What's going on?" he asked. "Mr. Thompson said your granddaughter is missing? She can't be. I swear I've been out there the entire time, keeping watch."

"I begged you to be extra vigilant. You sure you weren't on your phone or playing video games, or maybe you left to get a caramel chocolate whipped creme latte with extra foam?" I asked accusingly.

"No sir!" the officer said.

"Now, Howie." Sammy tried to calm me down. "I'm sure there's a logical explanation here."

"My granddaughter has been kidnapped by an arsonist who's out for revenge! I will not be calm!" I shouted.

"Kidnapped?" the officer gasped.

"Howie. Let's consider this. There's no evidence of forced entry. There was no struggle here."

"Well, maybe it was someone she knew, and she just let them in the front door. Is there something you aren't telling me?" I rounded on the officer.

"Sir, I understand why you're upset, but I swear to you I haven't taken my eyes off your house, and there hasn't been a soul in or out of the front door."

Officer Benson and I glared at each other while he radioed the station to let them know Ellie was missing. A cold dread settled over me while my heart pounded like a relentless drum. My mind raced with terrifying scenarios, each more horrifying than the last, leaving me with a suffocating sense of helplessness. Fear gnawed at my insides, and every second felt like an eternity as I struggled to stay focused and think of what to do next.

"Is it possible she slipped out the backdoor to meet a friend?" Sammy asked. "What about the EMT you said was flirting with her and listening to your conversation at the accident scene?"

"She would never do that to me!" I insisted.

"But wouldn't Scooby have raised a ruckus if someone broke in? I've heard that dog bark when he's upset. It's unbelievably loud. Officer Benson would have heard it, too."

"Maybe they poisoned him, and he was sleeping," I suggested wildly.

When we all turned to look at Scooby, he barked and wiggled around like he thought he was getting a treat or a walk.

"Scooby wasn't poisoned," Sammy pointed out. "I think Detective Rodriguez is right. You're getting too personal about this."

"They're sending an additional squad car right over," Officer Benson said.

"I swear if anything happened to her, I'm holding you personally responsible!" I snapped.

When the officer's phone rang, I glared at him. "That better be important!"

"It's Detective Rodriguez," he responded. "Officer Benson," he said into the phone. "Yes. No. Yes. Yes, ma'am. She wants to talk to you," he insisted, handing me the phone.

I braced myself, hoping for the best and dreading the worst. "Detective," I said, holding my breath, waiting to hear the news.

"Ellie was arrested."

Chapter 12

"I obviously didn't hear you right. Who was arrested?" Surely, she said someone else's name. She didn't just tell me it was my granddaughter.

"*Ellie*," she stated clearly.

"What on earth for?" I moaned.

"She was caught up in a sweep of protestors vandalizing an administration building on campus."

What was happening here? First, she snuck out of the house, evading her police protection, and now she has been arrested? I still couldn't believe my own ears. "Protestors?" I'm practically shrieking, I'm so upset. I had already experienced a wild roller coaster ride of emotions over my missing granddaughter, and now this? I had hit my limit. "What in blazes were they protesting?"

"Detective O'Sullivan, you need to control yourself. Why don't you come down to the station so we can discuss this like calm, rational adults?"

"Oh, I'm rational, all right. You tell my granddaughter she's grounded until she's 40!" I shouted before stabbing the disconnect button. Remember when we had landlines, and we could slam the phone down, and the other person knew it? Yeah, I miss those days. Poking a screen extra hard with my finger did nothing for me.

"Let's go!" I snapped at Sammy while Scooby waited across the room with a confused expression. He's never seen me this angry. "Scooby, I apologize," I told him calmly. At least *he* behaves. Most of the time, anyway. "We'll be back shortly." He's disappointed he can't be a part of whatever the excitement is, but he should thank his lucky stars he didn't have any strong-willed grandchildren.

When we arrived at the police station, a smartly dressed young man with short, neatly combed brown hair and wire-rimmed glasses greeted us in the lobby. "Detective O'Sullivan, Mr. Thompson." He nodded at us. "I'm Ronnie, an assistant for the detectives. Right this way," he insisted in a crisp and efficient manner. It's a good thing someone is calm here, I thought. "The moment they brought the protestors in, I recognized your granddaughter and placed her in an empty office."

"I appreciate that," I told him. "Can you tell me what's going on? How did this happen?"

"Well, sir, I'm not supposed to..." he stammered.

"Just tell me!" I shouted.

"Howie..." Sammy cautioned.

"Please!" I added.

Ronnie scanned the area, making sure we were alone, his voice dropping to a whisper. "Marah Sterling led a protest at the college--"

"Hold on. Marah Sterling, the radical activist who is one of our suspects?" I asked.

"Yes, sir. They were protesting the 4th of July Festival."

"What are you laughing about?" I barked at Sammy, who was clearly trying to control his mirth.

"The apple doesn't fall far from that tree, does it?" he pointed out.

"Excuse me?"

"Howie, if you were thinking clearly, you'd remember that Ellie *knew* Sterling was a suspect. She must have learned of the protest while we were gone, so she snuck out to investigate on her own."

I paused, dumbfounded at his assessment. He was right. Ellie would never consider it appropriate to take part in a protest that involved vandalism. Unless, of course, she thought it would help me solve a case. But I was still unhappy about it. She took a huge risk by leaving the house. *And* by investigating a suspect on her own.

"Call Jack," I told Sammy.

"But he's an intellectual property rights lawyer," Sammy pointed out.

"I get that. Just call him. He'll know what to do. She may have done it for what she *thought* were the right reasons, but she still got arrested, and I want Jack's advice."

"Detective, can I see you, please?" Rodriguez appeared in front of us with a severe frown on her face.

"Of course," I said, dutifully following her down the hallway, leaving Sammy and Ronnie behind. She was not happy.

"Sit down," she said after leading me into an interrogation room, holding up her hand to stop me before I could even open my mouth to offer some sort of convoluted explanation. "I guess going rogue on an active investigation runs in the family."

"So I've been told." I flinched.

"I know we touched briefly on Marah Sterling yesterday, but is there anything you have to add? Anything you mighthave recalled since then that could help with the investigation?"

"Nothing earth-shattering. The festival committee members have had numerous discussions with her over the years, and we've made several accommodations, like giving Green Horizons League an educational booth at the event, placing recycling bins throughout the park, and using as many recyclable materials as we could, the whole nine yards. But every year, she insists it isn't enough, and the event should be canceled. Have you questioned her since the arrest? What did she say?"

"She isn't in custody."

"Seriously? Why not? You arrest my granddaughter and the rest of the protestors but not the ring leader?"

"Detective O'Sullivan, you've been warned repeatedly about taking this too personally, and while you may be able to throw your weight around with my officers, it won't work with me."

"I get it. I apologize. I will control myself. But, please, I'm confused about why you didn't take Marah Sterling into custody."

"She took off when we showed up. We don't know where she is, but we're looking for her," she explained.

"Oh. Okay." Now I'm embarrassed.

"There's something else I have to tell you. Derrick Harland is dead."

"How do you know?"

"Ronnie, my assistant who you met in the lobby, checked with the National Criminal Database, and it showed that Harland was killed two years ago in January in Minnesota after his car skidded off a bridge and plunged into Lake Superior while being chased by the Minnesota Highway Patrol.

"Why were they chasing him? Wait. Let me guess. Arson suspect."

She nodded. "The record said his car sank almost immediately."

"I've often thought over the years that he could be dead, but now we know. I wonder what he was doing in Minnesota? Other than starting fires, of course. So that eliminates one of our suspects. But I have to ask. What happens to Ellie now? I mean, she has to face the consequences for her actions, but I'm concerned with the threats against us that she'd be unsafe here in lockup."

"I understand that, and we're releasing her into your custody for the time being."

"I appreciate that."

"And now I have to go," Detective Rodriguez said, glancing at her watch, "because I have a meeting I have to get to. You can pick up Ellie in the lobby."

"Thanks. I appreciate it, Detective. And I promise to control myself from now on."

"Yes. Of course," she said, but I don't think she believed me.

After she left, with all the excitement that had gone down, I realized I had forgotten to ask her how the meeting with the mayor went.

When I returned to the lobby, Ellie, Jack, and Sammy were waiting for me.

"Gramps, I'm so sorry!" Ellie exclaimed the moment she saw me.

I couldn't decide whether to hug her or lecture her. I wanted to do both but didn't know where to start. "What were you thinking?" I blurted out.

"I--" she started.

I cut her off because, obviously, I wasn't actually looking for an answer, and the urge to yell at her overrode my worry. "Ronnie and Detective Rodriguez told me you went to the Marah Sterling protest, and your friend Sammy here tried to defend you because he thinks you take after me, but have you forgotten? Someone ran you off the road! Possibly Marah Sterling! Who knows what they might do next? And if you think I'm mad, imagine what your mother will say. You'll be lucky if she doesn't put you on the next available plane!" Meanwhile, people in the lobby stared at us with fascination and horror. "The least you could have done was leave a note. I thought you were kidnapped!"

"Gramps, I was just about to text you when I got arrested, I swear! Look, I know you're mad, but you need to hear me out."

After all that, she was still trying to justify her outlandish and risky behavior. What was it with kids these days?

"Listen to her, Howie." Jack rolled between us.

"Go ahead," I told her.

"I got bored waiting for you to come back from wherever it was you went this morning."

I cringed at that, remembering our escapade and how mad Rodriguez was. Maybe Sammy was right. Maybe my granddaughter did take after me. But I was still mad.

Ellie continued, "You told me Marah Sterling was a suspect, so I decided to do a little digging on my own.

Wouldn't you know it? She announced on her social media channels that she was leading a protest against the festival on campus today, so I decided it was the perfect opportunity to infiltrate her group. You know, to see if I could learn anything."

I still couldn't decide if I should be mad or impressed. I was a little of both, I suppose.

"How on earth did you get out of the house undetected? I hope you know that Officer Benson is in big trouble for neglecting his duties."

"Oh no! I never meant to make trouble for him. I take full responsibility. I snuck out the backdoor, climbed the neighbor's fence, walked over two blocks, and then Braden picked me up and drove me to campus. Turns out I'm reallygood at sneaking around. There's no way Officer Benson could have known what I did."

Lovely. My granddaughter just admitted she was good at being sneaky. "Uhhh, who's Braden? You've never mentioned this name before. Is he one of Sterling's activists?"

"Oh no, nothing like that. He's the paramedic I met at the accident scene. But more importantly, I gathered some essential information. Information that I think proves Marah Sterling is the arsonist. I overheard Marah saying that she had it on good authority the festival was about to be canceled because of the fires. Then the person she was talking to said, 'so our plan is working?' and she responded, 'big time!' Don't you see? Marah and her gang are behind the fires!" she said, looking at me hopefully.

"I'm not sure it's that cut and dry, but obviously, Detective Rodriguez will investigate this further. Assuming they find Sterling, that is. But for now, I suggest we head home before we wear out our welcome here. Hey, Sarge," I asked the desk sergeant on duty, "Are we free to go?"

"Yes, sir!" he responded.

"Wait." Ellie grabbed my arm and pointed at the TV hanging in the lobby. We installed it many years ago to keep people entertained and distracted while they were waiting. It actually worked quite well at taming impatient citizens, but I almost forgot it was there. We stood in the lobby, our eyes fixed on the television screen, staring at the mayor, who was holding a press conference.

"Good afternoon ladies and gentlemen of Boulder," he began, his tone measured and reassuring, "due to recent events, and out of an abundance of caution, we have made the difficult decision to cancel this year's 4th of July Festival."

Even though I wasn't surprised, my heart sank to my feet. What a disappointment.

"While I want to assure everyone that there is no immediate public danger, our priority is always the safety and well-being of our town. We are working closely with law enforcement to ensure that all threats are thoroughly investigated." He paused, offering a practiced, sympathetic smile. "We understand how important this festival is to our city, and we share your disappointment. But please know, this decision was made with the utmost consideration for your safety. Thank you for your understanding and cooperation."

At that, the screen cut back to I Love Lucy, the program that was running before the mayor's announcement. The weight of the mayor's words hung heavily in the room.

"That blows," Ellie groaned.

Chapter 13

As we left the police station, the weight of the day settled heavily on my shoulders. Ellie looked worn and frazzled but relieved to be going home. "How are we going to explain this to your mother?" I asked.

"I was hoping you would..." she trailed off.

"Oh, no, missy, this is all on you!"

"What if we just don't tell her?" she suggested.

"What if she sees it on the news?"

"In Florida?"

"You never know. Boulder often makes the news," I reminded her. "By the way, we're taking you back to your apartment to pack a suitcase," I said firmly, my voice brooking no argument.

Ellie opened her mouth to protest, but I cut her off. "I know the festival was canceled, and I hope for the community's sake that means everyone is safe, but the arsonist is still out there, and until we catch whoever it is, you're staying with me. And no sneaking out this time."

Sammy nodded in agreement, his usual easygoing demeanor replaced with a steely resolve. "He's right, Ellie. It's not safe. You need to stay where we can keep an eye on you."

Ellie sighed, her shoulders slumping in resignation. "Okay, Gramps. But just for a little while, right?"

"We'll see," I replied, not wanting to make promises I couldn't keep. "Your safety is the most important thing right now."

As we reached Sammy's pickup, I opened the back door for Ellie. She slid in without further protest, her eyes reflecting a mix of exhaustion and resignation. Sammy got behind the wheel, and I took the passenger seat, both of us instinctively watching the surroundings for any signs of danger.

The drive to Ellie's apartment was quiet, the tension palpable. The typically lively streets of Boulder also seemed eerily quiet. People had heard the news and were staying inside. The festival cancellation weighed heavily on my mind, a bitter pill to swallow for a town that cherished the event. My heart ached for the families and children who looked forward to this day all year. But as Sammy drove quietly along our somber streets, I couldn't shake the worry gnawing at my gut, hoping that the person who had made the threats would relent now that their demands were met. Yet, skepticism clung to me. Would canceling the festival be enough? If not, then what?

Once we arrived, I followed Ellie up to her apartment, while Sammy stayed outside to keep an eye on things from there. Ellie quickly gathered her essentials, throwing clothes and toiletries into a suitcase with practiced efficiency. "Don't worry about the rest," I told her. "We can come back for anything else later."

As she zipped up her suitcase, she glanced at me, a flicker of defiance in her eyes. "I can take care of myself, you know."

"I know you can," I said gently, "but this isn't just about you. It's about keeping *everyone* safe, including you. We're stronger together, Ellie. Just humor an old man, okay?"

She gave a small smile and nodded. "Okay, Gramps. Let's go."

As we stepped out of the apartment building, my eyes caught a flicker of movement behind a tree across the street. "Hold on a second," I murmured, signaling Sammy and Ellie to stay put. I crossed the street and approached the tree cautiously, heart pounding, but when I reached it, no one was there. Just shadows and the rustle of leaves. I rubbed my tired eyes.

"It was nothing," I told an anxious-looking Sammy and Ellie. "Must be my imagination. It's been a long day. Let's get home and eat dinner," I said as we all climbed back into the truck, and I hoped for a quiet evening at home to regroup.

When we arrived home, we were met by the police escort which Detective Rodriguez insisted we keep out of an abundance of caution. No surprise, Scooby greeted us excitedly. He didn't care that Ellie was arrested. He was miffed however that we had been gone for so long and didn't include him in our adventures.

"Jack wants to know what he should pick up for dinner," I explained, reading the text message he just sent me.

As Sammy and I opened our mouths to say 'pizza,' Ellie beat us to the punch. "No pizza!" she scolded.

"Fine. Then you pick," I told her.

"What about sandwiches from Snarf's?" Sammy suggested.

"That sounds good," I said, looking to Ellie to make sure it was acceptable. Thankfully, she nodded in agreement, otherwise I feared we could be at this all night.

Of course, Jack didn't have to request Sammy's and my sandwich order because if there was one thing we liked almost as much as pizza, it was sandwiches. And we always got the same ones. Creatures of habit we were. He only had to ask what kind Ellie wanted. **She wants the avoca-**

do, sprouts, and provolone cheese sandwich. I texted back.

Seriously? How is that a proper sandwich? He responded.

Don't ask! I exclaimed.

"I'm sorry about the festival, man," Sammy said as we placed napkins and beer on the kitchen table, waiting for Jack to arrive.

"Yeah, me too," I replied. "Of course, I'm deeply disappointed. It's not just a loss for me. It's a loss for the community, and I hate that fear and uncertainty overshadowed the event. Still, I'd never forgive myself if we went ahead with the celebration and something horrible happened."

"I kind of understand the mayor's position. He was between a rock and a hard place, I guess you could say, huh?" Sammy pointed out.

Ellie shook her head. "If Sterling and her team really are behind the fires and the threats, it makes me mad that she got her way, you know? It isn't fair that by resorting to dishonest and illegal tactics, they finally got the festival canceled."

"We *will* find whoever is behind all of this, and next year, it will be bigger and better than ever," Sammy insisted.

"Yeah, I guess. It won't be the 100th anniversary, though," Ellie pointed out.

After that, the three of us sat in somber silence, the minutes ticking by as we waited for Jack to arrive with our sandwiches. The usual excitement of the holiday felt like a distant memory now. When Jack arrived, we scrambled to the door to greet him.

"I'm starving!" Sammy exclaimed.

"I saw your reporter friend in front of the sandwich shop," Jack said as he rolled through the door with Chance carrying the bag of sandwiches.

"What was she doing there?" I asked grumpily. Detective Rodriguez told me that after Kara's report from the second fire, the mayor complained that his office was overwhelmed with people calling and emailing, fearful that the town was in danger and furious that they hadn't been warned earlier. He said he had no choice but to cancel festival.

"She was doing those 'person on the street' interviews where people give their opinions."

"What were people saying?" I asked.

"It was mixed. Some were saying they thought it was best. Others said they felt like it should be up to the individual to decide. But one thing everyone agreed on: it won't seem like 4th of July without the festival."

"So now I have to ask, Mr. Lawyer..."

"Yes..." Jack smiled, obviously knowing where this was headed.

"Where do we go next with the charges against Ellie?"

"As Ellie assured me, she did not take part in spray painting the building..."

"Of course," I responded.

"And everyone there had their phones out filming it all."

"People film themselves committing a crime?" I asked, stunned.

"They sure do," he responded. "I'm going to assume someone has footage of Ellie *not* committing a crime and I'll ask that the charges against her be dropped. But that's really all I have so far."

"I appreciate your help on this Jack."

"Of course. And obviously I know the festival is canceled but I feel like I'm out of the loop on the updates. Care to clue me in? Where do things stand with our suspects?

"Mara Sterling is in the wind," I pointed out.

"They'll find her soon. I'm sure of it," he said.

"If she's the arsonist, maybe news of the cancellation will bring her out of hiding," Sammy suggested.

"We could hope."

"Speaking of going missing. Any updates on that Harland guy?" Jack asked.

"Yeah, get this. He's dead."

"Dead?" Sammy exclaimed.

"As a doornail."

"He finally double cross the wrong person?" Jack asked.

"Skidded off a bridge in Minnesota during a police chase and drowned."

"Why am I not surprised?" Sammy asked.

"Sammy and I followed Parot this morning," I added.

"I told you I didn't want to know about that," Jack reminded us.

"Oh, it's okay. Detective Rodriguez already knows all about it."

"You told her?"

"Kind of. When Parot managed to lose us so he could set the second fire and we arrived on the scene, Rodriguez demanded we tell her how we got there so fast, and because I was sure Parot started it, we had to admit we had been following him."

"Any clues at the fire scene?"

"There was a second note at the scene and another bottle of Maginni's lighter fluid."

"Another note? Aimed at you?"

"Unfortunately, yes," I said, showing him the picture. "But there's more. We saw Trent Baxter lurking nearby."

"The fire?"

"Yes."

"What did you do? Did you go after him?" Jack asked.

"No, unfortunately, we didn't have the chance. Rodriguez got a text from the mayor insisting she come to his office, so she made us swear we wouldn't follow Baxter."

"We have to find out what he was doing there. What if he was there to watch his handy work?" Jack suggested.

"I'm thinking about reaching out to his ex-wife to see if she'd be willing to answer some questions. She owns the Mountain Delights Coffee Shop in town."

"What if this is a two-person job?" Ellie asked.

"Like two of our suspects are working together?" Jack responded.

"Yes," Ellie replied. "What if Parot and Baxter teamed up to bring you and the festival down? What if the car chase was just a distraction? Parot didn't start the fire. He led you on a wild goose chase while Baxter set it."

"We saw Baxter drive away in a black SUV. He could have easily run Ellie off the road," Sammy suggested as he eagerly riffled through the bag of sandwiches.

"We better eat before Sammy here keels over from starvation," I pointed out. "But then I'll contact Marjorie Baxter to see if she'd talk to us."

"Sounds like a plan," Sammy said, opening and closing kitchen cupboard doors.

"The potato chips are in the cupboard closest to the fridge," I reminded him.

"Thank goodness! I can't eat a sandwich without chips," he exclaimed.

"We know!" the rest of us chorused.

Chapter 14

I was pleasantly surprised when Marjorie, Trent's ex-wife, agreed to see me. We're meeting at her coffee shop, even though Mondays were one of their busiest days, with everyone fueling up on caffeine to start the week, she said we could talk between customers. When Trent was first accused of stealing the jewelry, she took his side in his campaign against me. She, like Trent, felt it was my responsibility to publicly assert his innocence. But after some time passed, and Trent became more unhinged, Marjorie saw things differently. So, wasn't I surprised when she spotted me getting lunch at a popular food truck on a chilly fall day last year and apologized! Now, it was almost surreal to sit across from her over a cup of coffee, chatting about her ex-husband while the shop buzzed around us. "Detective O'Sullivan," she began, with a soft voice.

"Please, it's Howie. I've retired," I told her.

"Howie. I was surprised to get your call. And I'm worried that Trent's in trouble again."

"When was the last time you spoke with your ex?" I asked.

"Just yesterday, actually. Despite being divorced, we still talk often."

"What was his state of mind?"

She shrugged. "The usual. No matter what happens, it's always someone else's fault."

"What do you mean?"

"He won't take responsibility for anything. If he accidentally leaves his milk in the grocery cart because he's distracted, he complains to the store manager that someone should have noticed that and told him. I could go on, but I'm sure you get the gist."

"So he hasn't really changed since the last time I dealt with him."

She shook her head somewhat tearfully. "He spiraled so bad after he got fired."

I paused to sip my coffee. "This might sound surprising, but in a way, I don't blame him. I know how I'd feel if I had been unjustly accused of stealing, only to be cleared of any wrongdoing, yet still get fired."

She nodded. "Yes, you can certainly see *why* he'd be so angry about how he was treated. But, you know, lots of people catch unfair breaks in life and don't spin out of control for years on end."

I exhaled, guilt washing over me. "I truly wished I could have caught the guilty party. I hate that someone got away with stealing, and an innocent person was blamed. I never believed Trent stole the jewelry, but my job was only to investigate. Not publicly exonerate him. However, I might have done things differently if I had realized at the time that they would fire him anyway. I still urged the fire department to reinstate him, but unfortunately, my opinion on that matter didn't hold much weight. I guess, given the bad publicity they got in the beginning, the department felt he was too much of a liability in the long run. It was a complicated situation."

Marjorie nodded, turning an understanding eye my way. "I agree. And I turned against you, too, blaming you for what happened. But then Trent became impossible to live with. I begged him to go to counseling to get help. I even offered to go with him. He kept promising to change, to get better, but he never did. He continuously grew more resentful of the system and everyone in it." The pain in her eyes was evident as she recounted the past.

"I'm sorry you had to go through that. You were in a no-win situation."

"I was," she admitted. "Trent was a different person, so angry and bitter. He wasn't the man I married. I don't think he stole the jewelry either, and it was horribly unfair that they still fired him. But it consumed him, and he became obsessed with revenge."

I hesitated before asking the big question. After everything she had been through, she wouldn't appreciate what I was about to say. "I have to ask you a delicate question, and I hope you'll understand why."

"Go ahead."

"You've obviously heard about the fires at Boulder Memorial Park."

"Yes, and I'm heartbroken that the mayor canceled the 4th of July Festival." She winced. "My cafe always rents a booth there, and it's a huge money maker for us. Everyone wants their iced coffee drinks, of course. Plus, it's just so much fun. We look forward to it every year. And on top of that, now I'm out a lot of money and effort."

I braced myself for her reaction. "I'm just going to come out and ask because I don't know another way. Do you think Trent could have set those fires as payback? For the town, for me, and maybe even you?"

She paused, looking away for a moment. I was waiting for her to get angry and lash out at such an intrusive question, but I was shocked when she didn't. "I'm not sure, Howie. The Trent I knew ten years ago would never consider such a thing, but he's warped and unpredictable now. As much as I hate to say this, I think he's capable of just about anything."

"Would you tell me where I can find him? I'd really like to talk to him. Although I don't know that he'll want to talk to me."

"He has an apartment on 28th Street, and thankfully, he actually has a job now. He works at Maginni's Hardware, and from what I understand, he does a pretty good job there. His boss really likes him, and supposedly, he's considering making him an assistant manager. But if he actually set those fires, or even if he just gets accused, there's no telling how he'll react."

I tried my best to maintain a neutral expression when she said Trent was working at Maginni's. Of course, anyone could have bought lighter fluid there. It's the oldest, most popular hardware store in town. I can only imagine how many bottles they sell every summer. But still... "Okay, I'll check out Maginni's," I assure her. "And while I'm here, I have another question."

"Go ahead."

"What kind of car does he drive?" Yes, we already saw him in a black SUV, but I wanted to know what *she* said about it. For all I knew, he borrowed it from a friend just to run Ellie off the road and throw us off his trail.

"A black SUV. Funny you should ask about that. He told me he was involved in a minor accident on Saturday and had to take it to a body shop for repairs."

At that, I squeezed my coffee cup so hard that I splashed some onto my hand.

"Oh no! Be careful!" she said.

"Did he say how the minor accident happened?"

"Just that someone hit him, but he wasn't injured.'

"Which body shop did he take it to?"

"Sid's."

"I know that place. They do good work," I responded, trying desperately to maintain my cool.

"Howie, if you don't mind, I should probably get back to work now, my cashier is frantically signaling me. Would you let me know what you find out? I hate the idea of Trent committing a crime so horrendous as setting fire to something. I'd still like to think it's impossible, but I just don't know for sure."

"I really appreciate your time," I told her, shaking her hand. "I'll keep you updated as much as I can." If Trent truly is our arsonist and ran my granddaughter off the road, I won't be allowed to tell her much, but I understand why she's concerned.

After stepping outside the coffee shop, I phoned Sammy. "Hey, how about a trip to Maginni's Hardware?"

"Okay, what do you need?"

"I need to talk to Trent Baxter. His ex-wife said he's working there."

"You've got to be kidding me."

"Nope."

"Trent Baxter, a suspect in the fires that were started with lighter fluid from Maginni's works at Maginni's."

"Yes, sir."

Sammy whistles softly. "Doesn't that beat all?"

"There's more. She confirmed he drives a black SUV *and* was in a minor accident recently."

"Oh wow. I better go with you to keep you in check."

"Exactly."

"I'm about five minutes away. I'll be right there," Sammy said.

Three minutes later, Sammy screeched to a halt in front of the coffee shop.

"I got here as quick as I could, boss."

"No kidding!" I told him, barely getting my seat belt fastened before he sped away.

"So, the clues are pointing to Trent, huh?" he asked.

"It looks like it."

"Do you think he'll even talk to us?"

"I sure hope so. Marjorie said his SUV is at Sid's, which is where I had them take Ellie's car."

"That's convenient."

"That's what I thought-- Sammy," I interrupted myself, my voice low and tense.

"What's wrong?"

"We're being followed."

Chapter 15

Sammy's eyes darted to the side mirror, his jaw tightening as he surveyed the traffic behind us. "You want me to shake him?"

"You see it too? It's not just me?"

"The dark sedan, two cars behind," he said.

"That's what I thought." Drat. I hoped I was just being paranoid. "Don't get too crazed. I don't want him to know we've spotted him. Make a couple of random turns to see what he does. But don't make it obvious."

Sammy turned right on Valmont Road, and so did the sedan. When he made a left on 30th Street, the sedan did the same. My heart pounded, adrenaline surging once again. "Make one more left at Glenwood Drive. If he does, too, we'll know he's following us."

Who could it be? Marcus Parot? Marah Sterling? Trent Baxter? Perhaps it's Trent, who spotted me talking to Marjorie and knew we were on to him. But when Sammy turned into the 7-11 on the corner, the sedan drove by without so much as a glance our way.

He chuckled nervously, "Guess we're just jumpy after everything that's happened."

"I hope that's all it is," I told him. Let's wait here a minute just to be certain." But after several minutes and no sign of the sedan, I told Sammy to head to Maginni's. It's more important than ever that we talk to Trent. And if he isn't there, does that mean he was the guy following us?

The automatic doors swooshed open as Sammy and I approached the store, transporting me instantly to a time when my dad and I shopped here, starting in the 1950s. From the earthy aroma of fresh-cut lumber to the sharp, metallic scent of steel tools to the more subtle whiff of rubber hoses and gaskets, this store has always caused sensory overload for me. But in a fun way. So many doo-dads and gadgets to behold in this 60,000 square foot building. It was a Boulder landmark. A visual feast for a DIYer like myself—a labyrinth of aisles lined with neatly organized shelves stretching from floor to ceiling in a stunning display of hand tools—hammers, screwdrivers, and wrenches—hanging in perfect rows...

"Howie? Howie?" Sammy interrupted my thoughts. "Daydream much?" he chortled.

"Huh? Oh! Sorry about that. It's hard not to daydream in this place."

"I get it, but we're here on official business, remember? Which department does Trent work in?"

"Oh. That's a good question." I was so lost in the charm of the hardware store I forgot for a moment that we were here to question a man who could have run my granddaughter off the road. "No clue." I wished I had thought of that beforehand. I should have asked Marjorie. In a store this big, who knew how long it might take to find him? Or if he's even working today. After Marjorie told me about his so-called minor accident, my brain kind of shut down, and I didn't think to ask.

We wandered down an aisle with a wall of neatly labeled drawers holding every type of screw, bolt, and nail imaginable while pegboards displayed hooks, fasteners, and other small hardware items in meticulous order. After that, we turned left onto the paint aisle - a riot of color, with countless cans lined up like soldiers, ready to tackle the home paint job.

"Look, there's a clerk," Sammy pointed out. "Maybe he knows Trent."

Thankfully, the clerk directed us to the gardening section, where we spotted Trent talking to two older women about what kind of fertilizer they should use in their gardens.

Seeing him again gave me a surprise jolt of anger and suspicion while old grudges bubbled back to the surface. The suspicion that he might be responsible for the fires and Ellie's accident fueled my resolve to uncover the truth.

To say *he* looked shocked and then displeased when he noticed our approach is the understatement of the year. His posture stiffened, while his expression was anything but welcoming.

"What do you want?" he growled.

If it were anybody else, we'd exchange pleasantries beforehand, but considering what this man may have done to my family, I was hardly in the mood.

"We'd like to talk to you about the fires at Boulder Memorial Park," I said.

"Are you serious?" he sneered. "You think I'm responsible for those fires? Man, you're a piece of work, aren't you? But why am I not surprised? I should have you thrown out of here on your ear," he said, taking a step toward me. For a second, I was convinced he was about to take a swing at me. That's okay. I'm used to it. He certainly wouldn't be the first suspect who tried to take his frustrations out on me. It would also confirm my suspicions that Trent Baxter was out of control.

Fortunately, Sammy stepped in, his voice steady. "We just want to know where you were when the floats burned down."

Trent crossed his arms over his chest, glaring daggers at us. "It's none of your business, but I was here at work."

I tilted my head at him. "But the first fire was started around 6:00, and Maginni's doesn't open until 8:00."

Trent huffed. "The 4th of July is our busiest time of the year. We all had to come in early and help with merchandise re-stocking. You can double-check with my boss if you don't believe me. Hey, why don't you do that so you could be two for two in getting me fired? Wouldn't you enjoy that?"

In my mind, I told myself that if he tried to harm Ellie, I'd do more than get him fired, but I restrained myself. Every suspect was still considered innocent until I could prove otherwise. "Actually, Trent, I *wouldn't* enjoy that. But what about the second fire? The one where the judges' stand burned down? The one where we saw you lurking in the crowd."

Trent's expression flickered between surprise and confusion, a mix that made it hard to decipher whether he was genuinely caught off guard or masking something more profound. We stood there for a moment, tension hanging thick in the air. But then a middle-aged man wearing a short-sleeve collared shirt with a tie and a friendly demeanor approached us. His name tag read Richard Brown, Store Manager.

"Is there a problem here?" he asked, looking between us.

As much as I wanted to tell him we were arresting an arsonist, I didn't. Trent looked awfully suspicious, and I was starting to think that Ellie could be right—two of our suspects might be working together, but I would hate to ruin this job for him if he wasn't our guy. I forced a smile. "No problem. We were just talking to Trent about the best grill to get for the 4th of July."

The boss looked relieved, nodding. "Well, Trent knows his stuff. Let me know if you need any help."

Baxter looked surprised and yet relieved that we didn't say anything further to his boss. If he was guilty, I would get him. It was only a matter of time.

"I have to get back to work so I don't lose this job too," he announced before hurrying away, halting any further questions, which I thought was awfully convenient for him.

"We'll be in touch," I muttered as we watched him disappear around a corner.

When we headed toward the exit, Sammy nudged me, pointing to a large display of lighter fluid for sale.

"I see it, Sammy," I said as we walked to his pickup. "I see it."

"You mentioned that Trent's ex-wife said his SUV is at Sid's Auto Body?" Sammy reminded me.

"Yes. It's where I took Ellie's car too."

"So, maybe we take a detour there to check on Ellie's car..." Sammy trailed off.

"That's exactly what I was thinking, old friend."

Chapter 16

Sid's Auto Body Repair Shop hummed with activity, as always. It was a constant melody of industrial sounds, from the continuous clanging of metal to the whirr of power tools and the occasional hiss of a pneumatic wrench. Bright overhead lights cast a stark, white glow on the myriad of cars in various states of repair. The shop smelled of motor oil with a touch of fresh paint and a dash of burnt rubber.

I approached Sid with a grin, calling out, "Sid!"

Sid and I go way back, and he's the best auto body repair man in Boulder. That's why I didn't hesitate to tell the tow truck driver to take Ellie's car here. It's also undoubtedly why Trent brought his car here. But that may be his downfall.

"Howie, my man!" he exclaimed while we exchanged the handshake-half hug that seemed to be the thing now. I'm old enough to remember when men just shook hands.

Now we have to shake hands and clap each other on the back. It's kind of weird, but I go with it.

"How's retirement treating you?" he asked.

"I keep trying to retire, but it keeps sucking me back in."

Sid nodded. "Did you come here to check on Ellie's car? We're just getting started on it."

"I'm actually here about a different car. An SUV that belongs to Trent Baxter."

Despite Sid's confused expression, he answered right away. "It's over here," he said, leading me to the opposite side of the shop. "We just finished repairing it. He got rear-ended the other day."

"Rear-ended?" I asked. Now, I was the one who was confused. How did he get rear-ended by running into Ellie's car?

"Yeah. He didn't get hit that hard," he explained as he walked us around to the back end, pointing to a shiny new bumper.

"That's not what I was expecting," I told him.

"He was rear-ended at an intersection. Truthfully, that makes it sound worse than it was. He stopped for a red light before turning right. The driver behind him wasn't paying attention and didn't hit him that hard, but he had a towing hitch on the front of his jeep, and it poked a hole in Trent's bumper."

I circled the vehicle to check for a Green Horizons League sticker but couldn't find one.

"Hey, how is Ellie doing, by the way?" Sid asked.

"Huh? Oh, she's good," I responded distractedly. "Say, did you happen to get any other SUVs in but with front-end damage?"

"Hold on a sec. Are you looking for the vehicle that ran into Ellie? Didn't they stop?"

"It's a long story. But if you do see a vehicle matching that description, could you give me a shout? Without letting the vehicle owner know?"

"Sure thing."

"Okay, thanks."

"Always good to see you." Sid grinned and shook my hand again.

"Where to next, boss?" Sammy asked.

"You know what? I'm going home to mow my lawn. It's starting to look like a jungle, and I need a break from all of this madness. I need to clear my mind, and yardwork always calms me down."

"That may be the best idea you've had all day." Sammy smiled at me.

"You've got to be kidding me!" an angry voice from behind us exclaimed. "What are you doing here?"

"Uhhh, Howie," Sammy stammered as I turned toward the voice and came face to face once again with Trent Baxter.

"We're here checking on my granddaughter's car. What are *you* doing here?" I asked.

"I'm picking up *my* SUV."

"Okay, well." I wasn't sure what to say next.

"My ex-wife said she talked to you."

"She did."

"Do you really think I set those fires?" he asked, his voice dripping with disdain.

"Well, now that you're here and asking, I know you said you were at work when the floats were burned, but when I asked you about the fire at the judging stand, you didn't answer."

"I shouldn't have to answer *any* of your questions," he paused while I prepared for him to tell me off, but when his shoulders sagged I was caught off guard, "but I appreciate you not telling my boss why you were really at Maginni's. I'm trying to do a good job there and if he thought you were questioning me about the fires, well, I could lose my job."

"I'm just trying to get to the truth here, okay?" I pleaded.

"Fine. I was at the Sunshine Sandwich Shop across the street when the judge's stand burned down. I was curious about what was going on." He shrugged. Along with the *crowd* of people who were watching. I take it you aren't questioning *them* about setting the fire?"

"If I had reason to, I would," I told him. "Do you have a receipt for your purchase at the sandwich shop?"

"I didn't get a receipt because I paid with my credit card. Now, if you don't mind, I'm here to pick up my vehicle," hesaid before turning and walking off.

"Do you believe him?" Sammy asked.

"I don't know what to believe anymore," I responded.

After leaving Sid's, I called Detective Rodriguez to update her on what we'd learned about Trent. I also asked her to contact Maginni's to verify Trent's alibi that he was at work when the floats were destroyed.

"Hey, one more favor," I asked. "Don't mention his name specifically. If you could just get a list of everyone who allegedly clocked in at 5 AM that day, I think that would be helpful."

"Why get a list of everyone?" she asked.

"Look, I may not like the guy, but there's no use in singling him out *again* if he's truly innocent. If he's doing as well there as he and Marjorie claim and is trying to get a fresh start, I don't want to be the one to take that away."

"You're a good guy, O'Sullivan."

"Let's just hope for his sake he's telling the truth."

Chapter 17

Call me weird, but I actually enjoyed yard work. With Ellie working in the bookstore on campus today, accompanied by her police protection of course, I had time to putter around my yard. As I wheeled the lawnmower out of the garage, the familiar weight of it was almost comforting, and for a bit, it quieted my mind. I pushed it to the edge of the lawn with the sun on my back and a slight breeze wafting across the yard; I took a deep breath, then I did like I always do: checked the gas level, adjusted the choke, and with a firm pull on the starter cord, the engine roared to life, ready to tackle the overgrown grass I'd been neglecting. The lawnmower's hum and the warm summer sun settled me as I pushed the mower across the yard, breathing in the scent of freshly cut grass. Summer smells were the best. Nothing beats grass, barbeque, and beer. The rhythmic motion of crisscrossing the lawn was meditative, and I appreciated it. But just as I made another pass across the yard, my gaze drifted toward the bushes bordering my neighbor's property. I swore I saw a flicker of movement from the corner of my eye—a shadow that shouldn't have been there. I know, I know, lately, I've been seeing things that weren't there, but I was sure I just saw something.

Yes. There it was again. Something was out of place. My heart skipped a beat, the tranquility of the moment shattered. When I shut off the mower, the sudden silence was almost deafening. I wiped the sweat from my brow before peering intently at the bushes. The shadow moved. Fiddlesticks. I knew it was real. Someone was hiding from me! Every muscle in my body tensed as I glanced back at the patrol car behind me. I should march over there, insisting the officer check it out. Instead, I headed straight for the bushes. Someone had been following me, and it was time to put it to rest once and for all. It was a man! Holy smokes, it was Marcus Parot. I knew it! And now he was running.

"This ends here," I declared as adrenaline surged through me. I sprinted after him and launched myself airborne, tackling him to the ground with a force fueled by anger and frustration. He thrashed and struggled beneath me, desperately trying to break free. His elbow caught my ribs, knocking the wind out of me for a moment, but I held on, driven by the urgency of the situation. Officer

Tremont ran to us, shouting into his radio that we'd apprehended Marcus Parot at the O'Sullivan house and to send backup. Together, we struggled to hold him down while the officer snapped cuffs onto his wrists before dragging him to his feet.

"You're under arrest," he declared as Marcus finally stopped fighting us, a look of disbelief and resignation covering his face.

"I knew it was you!" I bellowed. "I never bought the redemption story your parole officer was trying to feed us. I should have known. Once a criminal, always a criminal."

"No! No! You don't understand. I just wanted a chance to explain and apologize!" Parot exclaimed.

"You want to explain setting fires and running my granddaughter off the road? You could have killed her! You could have killed anyone with your stunts! And you've been stalking me. There's nothing to explain. You're going back to jail, and you'll stay there this time," I told him.

"I swear, you have it all wrong. This is the first time I've tried to approach you!"

"Like I'm going to believe a thing you say," I scoffed.

"Let's go, buddy," Officer Tremont insisted, hauling him toward the patrol car.

"I want to thank you," Parot claimed as I followed them.

"Thank me? What are you talking about?" I stopped in the middle of the sidewalk. What an odd thing to say.

"Prison was the best thing that ever happened to me."

"Okay, now I *know* you're lying," I told him.

"Really! I mean it. It forced me to confront who I was and what I'd done. I got my GED. Then, I became an ordained minister. I've changed, and all I want to do now is help others like me—you know, counseling ex-prisoners."

To my great shock, something inside me shifted, and despite my years of dealing with deceitful criminals, a teeny tinypart of me wanted to believe him. His eyes held a sincerity I hadn't seen before, shocking me with a surprising spark of trust.

He must have seen the shift in my demeanor because he continued, even as Officer Tremont was pushing him into the car. "For me, prison wasn't just about punishment. It was about reflection and change. I spent a lot of time thinking about my life and the choices I made. Thank God the prison chaplain saw something in me. He saw me as a real person, not just a criminal. He pushed me to take responsibility for my actions and to better myself. I found purpose in helping others, in guiding them away from the mistakes I made."

Just as Officer Tremont closed the door, a car screeched to a halt in front of us, followed by a second patrol car.

"Excuse me! Excuse me! I'm Gavin Colle, Mr. Parot's parole officer," he exclaimed, showing me his badge. "What happened? What's going on?"

"I found Marcus Parot hiding in my bushes, that's what happened."

"Please, Officer, can I talk to Mr. Parot?" he asked.

Officer Tremont hesitated and looked to me before I nodded in agreement. He was in cuffs and surrounded by law enforcement, so it wasn't like we were in immediate danger.

"Mr. Parot," Officer Colle said, "I told you this wasn't how we do this, and we had to go through official channels to get permission for you to speak with Mr. O'Sullivan."

"I know," Parot said, hanging his head. "I was just so eager to apologize and thank him for helping change my life."

"Detective O'Sullivan," Colle turned to me, "I know what you must be thinking, and I know this isn't protocol, but while we're all here, please, just hear us out. I promise you I can answer any questions you might have."

I narrowed my eyes at him. "I find that unlikely, but okay, I'll bite. Can you tell me where he was when the floats were burned to the ground?"

"I can. He was leading an early morning Bible study for the men's addiction group at the Boulder United Church."

"Do you have any proof of that? Other than the men who were allegedly there? How about independent confirmation?"

"*I* was there supervising him," Officer Cole said. "We arrived around 5:00, and the meeting went from 6:00 to 8:00. Afterward, Mr. Parot stuck around and talked to those needing further advice. He did that until 9:00. Well within the time frame of the fires."

"Okay, then, what about the second fire? When the judge's stand was destroyed?"

"You mean when you were following him?"

Gulp. "Yes," I admitted reluctantly.

"He called me while it was happening. He thought it was some old prison buddies following him because he's received threats from former friends who didn't like that he was now counseling ex-convicts. He was convinced it was one of them who was following him. I insisted he drive straight to my office where we could meet, so that's what he did. When we learned it was you, I encouraged him to file a complaint or even a lawsuit. I wanted him to talk to an attorney, but he refused. Since then, he's been pushing to talk to you in person, but I told him we don't do that and that he must go through the proper channels to arrange a meeting and not just show up at your house!" Officer Colle glared at him. "Now, unfortunately, *you*, Detective, have every right to file a complaint for harassment and trespassing. Mr. Parot may be guilty of bad judgment by approaching you today, but I guarantee he didn't set those fires."

"You swear this is the first time you've tried to approach me?" I asked.

"Yes, sir," Parot nodded enthusiastically.

"All right. Let him go, officer. I don't think he's our arsonist."

After the officer unlocked the handcuffs, I pointed at Marcus. "Don't make me regret this."

"I swear, you'll never see me again, Mr. O'Sullivan," he said. "And thank you. For everything."

"I'll take you back to my office," Officer Colle told Marcus. "We have some paperwork to fill out on the incident."

I heaved a sigh as they drove away. There went my number one suspect.

Chapter 18

After the excitement died down and everyone left, I decided I could use a beer—the lawn would remain unfinished for now. I grabbed a bottle from the refrigerator and planted myself on the porch swing while Scooby hopped onto the chair across from me. "What do you think, Scoobs? Wild day, huh?"

He responded by circling on the chair several times to get comfortable, then plunked down with a loud dachshund sigh and promptly fell asleep—a quality I greatly admired in him.

Parot had a solid alibi, and as reluctant as I was to admit it, I found him sincere, which narrowed our suspect list to Marah Sterling and Trent Baxter. With Marah missing and Trent claiming to have two legitimate alibis, what was next? As I pondered Parot's transformation, I wondered about Derrick Harland. What did he do after he left Boulder, but before he was killed? Aside from continuing to set fires anyway. Perhaps the Minnesota Highway Patrol would share information with me about that fateful night? While I continued to sip my beer, I searched my phone for contact information for the MHP. Would they even take my call? The worst they could say is no, right?

"Minnesota Highway Patrol, this is Carol; how may I direct your call?"

"Hi there, I'm retired Detective Howard O'Sullivan from the Boulder Colorado Police Department, and I'm calling about a man named Derrick Harland. I realize this might be a long shot, but we investigated him for arson many years ago, and then he disappeared. But I've recently learned that he died. I hoped to get a few more details to close out my case file. Who would I speak to about that?"

"Certainly, Detective. Let me check our records," Carol responded politely. I waited while listening to the keys click-clacking on her keyboard. "I've got that record right here, and that would be Detective Barnes, but he's out right now. Should I have him call you?"

"Yes, please, that would be great."

"Okay. The message will appear in his inbox, and I'm sure he'll call you as soon as he can."

"Thanks so much!" I told her just as my phone flashed with a notification that Detective Rodriguez was calling. She must have learned about the Parot incident. I'll be getting an earful about chasing him down by myself, no doubt.

"Good afternoon, Detective!" I exclaimed like I had no idea why she was calling.

"We arrested Marah Sterling," she said without fanfare.

I guess I *didn't* know why she was calling!

"On what charges?" I asked.

"Arson, vandalism, evading law enforcement, threats... it's a lengthy list."

"What about running Ellie off the road?" I asked.

"We're still working on that one."

"But you have proof that she started the fires?"

"So far, it's circumstantial, but I expect to have more on it shortly. I may regret asking, but would you like to come down to the station?"

"You want me to interrogate her?" I asked in shock.

"Now, I didn't say that. But I'm willing to let you watch from the observation room."

"Okay. I'll be right there!" I exclaimed.

Detective Rodriguez met me at the front door of the police station. "You know you have to behave yourself, right?"

"I figured as much," I responded.

"I mean it. Control yourself, or I'll toss you. I'm allowing you to watch from the observation room as a professional courtesy, but I won't hesitate to have an officer escort you out if you get disruptive."

"I'll be on my best behavior," I told her. "Scout's honor. And I'm sure you heard about what happened with Marcus Parot."

"I did, and we'll discuss that later."

See, I knew she would scold me for that. "I know you're eager to get back to interrogation, but real quick, what about Trent Baxter's alibi? Were you able to confirm whether he was really working on Saturday morning? You know, Ellie had an interesting theory. She thought two of the suspects could be working together. Is it possible Sterling and Baxter were acting as a team?"

"It's an interesting theory," Detective Rodriguez acknowledged, "but so far, the evidence doesn't confirm it. Maginni's Hardware gave me a list of employees who punched in for the day, and Trent worked an 8-hour shift starting at 5 AM on the day in question and only checked out for lunch at 11:30," Detective Rodriguez added.

"But what about the receipt from the sandwich shop?" I pressed.

"Credit card receipts show Trent purchasing a turkey club sandwich combo meal with a side of potato chips and coleslaw at roughly the same time the fire started."

"I guess that answers that, huh?" I told her.

"That's actually why we arrested Marah Sterling."

"I'm not following."

"After you asked me to confirm Trent's alibi with his boss at Maginni's, it got me thinking."

"About?" I asked, still not understanding where she was going with this.

"I asked Mr. Brown, the store manager if he knew of anyone recently purchasing unusual amounts of lighter fluid."

"And?" I asked. "Hang on a second," I interrupted before she could answer. "He willingly gave you all this information? Is he allowed to do that?"

"Let's just say that Mr. Brown had some unpaid parking tickets that may have quietly gone away."

"Detective!" I exclaimed. "That's something I would do. Am I rubbing off on you?"

"I'm answering that with a 'no comment.'"

I smirked. I was glad I could provide some guidance here, even if it involved bending the rules a bit. "Let me guess. It wasn't Trent."

"Nope. When Mr. Brown questioned his cashiers, one of them recalled a *woman* who matched Marah Sterling's description who purchased a dozen bottles only a week ago. The cashier said she didn't seem like the type to buy lighter fluid at all, much less a dozen bottles."

"And?" I'm trying my hardest to stay calm as I ponder the fact we finally have our perpetrator in custody.

"She got very nervous and told him it was none of his business."

"Why do I get the sense there's more?"

"Because there is. I remembered seeing a bank directly across the street from where the floats were burned."

"Security cameras!" I exclaimed.

"You got it."

"Don't tell me the bank manager had parking tickets too."

"No." She smiled. "He was happy to turn over footage because he's concerned about fires that close to his bank."

"Are you saying we have footage of Marah Sterling setting fire to the floats?"

"No. Not quite. But we do have video of a woman in a Green Horizons League hoodie, matching Marah's height and weight, lurking near the float area shortly before the fire started."

"Okay then. What are we waiting for?" I exclaimed.

Chapter 19

Through the glass in the observation room, I watched as Detective Rodriguez settled into the chair across from Marah Sterling. The small, dimly lit interrogation room always felt oppressively intimate to me. The atmosphere was normallythick with tension, but this time, it was odd to experience it not as a professional investigator but more for personal reasons.

Marah sat with her arms crossed, her expression defiant but tinged with anxiety. She was a slender, athletic-looking person with freckles and long blonde hair tied back in a braid. Her trendy glasses were bright green, and she wore what I would guess were eco-friendly fabrics in earthy tones and hiking boots as if she wanted to be ready at any moment for a hike or an outdoor protest. She didn't request a lawyer. She told Detective Rodriguez that innocent people don't need lawyers.

I turned up the speaker volume so I wouldn't miss a single word.

"You must know we have numerous witnesses who filmed you spray painting *Cancel the Festival* on an administration building on campus," Rodriguez started.

"So," Sterling responded.

"But then you ran away, leaving the rest of your followers to answer for the crime. You realize running from the police is just the beginning of the charges we're building against you, right?"

Sterling rolled her eyes as if this was all beneath her. "Here's the deal. I warn my activists beforehand to wear shoes they can run in and not wear loose clothing because it's too easy for the authorities to grab. I can't help it if they were slow enough to get caught."

"Seriously?" Detective Rodriguez asked.

"Our voices must be heard. Unfortunately, sometimes, the only way to get people to pay attention is to do something drastic. Besides, it's not like we broke anything. Spray paint can be removed, you know."

"We have a witness who overheard you telling one of your staff that you had it on good authority the festival was about to be canceled because of the fires. That person responded with," Detective Rodriguez glanced down at her notes, "'soour plan is working?' and you responded with, 'big time!'" Rodriguez folded her hands together, staring at Sterling. "What did you mean by that?"

"It's true. I heard from a contact in the mayor's office that due to the negative publicity from the fires and Kara Belmont's brilliant reporting on the potential threats to the community, which I'll point out, the *police depart-ment* didn't publicize, the mayor was being pressured to cancel the festival."

"So you set the fires?" Rodriguez asked.

"What? No! Absolutely not!"

"But you just admitted your plans were working."

"I meant plans to get the festival canceled. But not through starting fires. I don't know what you think you have on me, but I guarantee it has nothing to do with any fires. That's not how we roll."

Detective Rodriguez leaned forward, her voice calm and firm. "Ms. Sterling, we have a witness who swears you purchased one dozen bottles of lighter fluid last week from Maginni's Hardware. Can you tell me why you needed twelve bottles of lighter fluid?"

Sterling's eyes grew wide with shock and indignation. "I've never bought lighter fluid in my life! I'm a vegan. Why would I need lighter fluid?"

Rodriguez raised an eyebrow, unfazed. "Vegan or not, the witness claims otherwise. How do you explain that?"

Marah shook her head vehemently. "I *can't* explain it. I don't know what to tell you, but I've never bought lighter fluid."

"Can you tell me where you were on Saturday at 6 AM?"

Sterling's eyes widened in a fleeting moment of panic while she opened and closed her mouth several times as if to form a quick, defensive reply, but her defiance was crumbling. She may have been adamant about the lighter fluid, but she sure wavered at *that* question.

"Let me help you with that," Rodriguez said, holding up an iPad in front of Marah's face. She pressed play, and the grainy security footage from the bank across the street appeared. It showed a figure resembling Marah slinking around the floats only moments before the fire broke out.

"I did not start those fires!" she exclaimed, pointing at the screen.

"If you didn't set the floats on fire, what were you doing there at that time of day? You obviously weren't a volunteer. You already admitted you wanted to get the festival canceled."

"Okay, okay, I admit it. I was there. But I did *not* set the floats on fire. Do you know how toxic that would be for the environment?"

"Then why *were* you there?" Rodriguez pressed.

"If you must know, I went there to slash the floats' tires. I figured if the parade got canceled, it would ruin everything else."

Detective Rodriguez glanced down at her notes, pretending to double-check them. But knowing her, she was setting the trap. Slowing everything down to make the suspect sweat. "But the tires were untouched," She finally responded, pointing it out in the file.

Sterling's story was unraveling, and it showed. She adjusted her glasses with trembling fingers before tightly crossing her arms as if to shield herself from the scrutiny. She was unable to meet Detective Rodriguez' piercing gaze, and her cheeks flushed. Her entire demeanor shifted from composed and confident to cornered and desperate, every movement reflecting the crumbling facade of her lies.

"Oh. You don't think... I mean... there's no way you think we'd actually... I admitted I was there to slash tires. But other than that and a little spray paint, that's all I'm guilty of... Hey! Wait!" she exclaimed, smacking her hand against the table. "I just remembered something. I saw someone. That's why I took off *before* I could slash the tires."

"Uh-huh. And can you describe this someone?" Rodriguez asked.

"I didn't get a good look. It was still dark out, and he was wearing a hat pulled down over his face, but I'm certain it was a man. And you know what? I remember smelling lighter fluid!"

"Yeah, right, likely story," I muttered.

Rodriguez's eyes narrowed, her voice taking on a sharper edge. "So you admit to being at the scene. And smelling lighter fluid. But you didn't light the match that set the floats on fire?" When Marah opened her mouth to respond again, Rodriguez held up her hand. "Never mind. You've already given your answer."

When I heard a knock on the interrogation room door, I worried it was Marah's attorney after all, and the questioning would be halted. But the door opened and it was Ronnie. "Detective." He nodded, handing her an official lookingdocument.

"Thank you," Rodriguez said before he nodded again and slipped out the door.

What could that be? Was that planned, or did he really have additional evidence? I can't see well enough to know what it is. Rodriguez turned the document over on the table while Sterling stared at it.

"Ms. Sterling, what kind of car do you drive?"

"What? Car? What?" she stammered.

"Just answer the question, please."

"I drive a Tesla," she claimed. "What else would I drive? And for the record, I ride my bike most places."

"You're telling me you don't have an SUV? A black SUV?"

"Of course not!"

"This vehicle registration says otherwise," Detective Rodriguez said, holding the document in front of her. "Tell me, were you recently involved in an accident?"

What is happening here? I'm so stunned, I don't know what to think. They found proof that Marah Sterling was driving the SUV that ran Ellie off the road?

"What? Vehicle registration? Let me see that," Sterling said, snatching the paper from her hand.

"This is not my vehicle! I've never seen this!"

"So you weren't driving the SUV that ran Ellie O'Sullivan's car off the road?"

"Who?"

"Ellie O'Sullivan."

"Who's that, and why would I try to run her off the road?"

"Because you've openly threatened her grandfather, Howard O'Sullivan, due to his involvement with the 4th of July Festival."

"I did no such thing!"

Sterling's eyes practically bug out of her head while her face pales even further. "I want my lawyer," she said as she folded her arms over her chest and pursed her lips.

After an officer escorted Sterling back to her holding cell, Detective Rodriguez joined me in the observation room.

"So, what's next?" I asked.

"We have enough to hold her for now on vandalism charges at the university and evading law enforcement. I'll continue working on the other charges. You must know we're working around the clock to solve this," Rodriguez assured me.

"We have to locate that SUV!" I exclaimed.

"I get that," she responded testily.

I paused to take a deep breath. "I know you're working this case thoroughly, and I have faith in you and the rest of the department," I told her.

"Thanks, O'Sullivan, I appreciate that."

I should have felt relief. Although the festival was canceled, the arsonist was in custody, and we were all safe. But as I left the precinct, I couldn't shake the feeling that we were missing a crucial piece of the puzzle, and time was running out.

Chapter 20

The following morning, I argued with Ellie about why I'd prefer she stay with me, at least through the holiday.

"Gramps, you told me you saw the evidence with your own eyes, and the festival was canceled, so we have nothing to worry about."

"How about you stay here for the holiday and we'll have our own little celebration? We'll invite the usual crew and you could invite some friends. Sid said your car will be ready this afternoon so we have to pick that up anyway."

"Oh, Braden said he'd take me."

Wonderful. How did this Braden character go from being a paramedic at the accident scene to hanging around my granddaughter so much? My detective instincts don't like it one bit, but I keep forgetting to ask Detective Rodriguez to run a background check on him.

"I'll take you to the bookstore of course," I told her grabbing the keys for my pickup.

"Oh, no need; Braden just pulled up."

"Shouldn't he come to the door? In my day, we knocked on the door like a proper gentleman."

"Gramps, it's not a date. He's just giving me a ride to work."

I watched as Ellie practically skipped down the sidewalk. Then I watched this Braden character, as I'd taken to calling him in my head, get out of the car and open the passenger door for her. Still not as good as coming to the door I harrumphed. And I still didn't trust him.

In fact, while I was thinking about it, it was time to call Detective Rodriguez but I was disappointed to get her voice mail. "Hey, Detective, any updates on Marah Sterling? Also, could you do an old man a favor and run a background check on a Braden Johnson for me? He's been hanging out with Ellie ever since the accident and I don't like it. I need to know if there's anything I should be concerned about."

As relieved as I'll be when Detective Rodriguez solidifies the case against Sterling, there's something about it that still doesn't sit right with me. Her last-minute claim about how she saw a man near the floats was awfully contrived.

But for argument's sake, let's say she did see a man there. A man who set the fires. Baxter, Parot, and Harland all have solid alibis. For different reasons, of course, but still... Is there someone we haven't thought of? I wracked my brain, trying to think of anyone else. I felt like there was a clue that was just out of reach. It was rattling around in my head, but I couldn't quite catch it. Ugh. I hated this!

When my phone rang, interrupting my thoughts, I was pleased to see the 218 area code. It must be the highway patrol from Minnesota.

"Howard O'Sullivan here."

"Detective O'Sullivan, this is Tim Ackerman from the Minnesota Highway Patrol. I'm sorry I wasn't available to take your call yesterday. I was in meetings most of the day."

"I can't say I miss that! Hey, I just had a couple of questions," I told him.

"Yes, you called about Derrick Harland. Sounds like you had some trouble with him back in the day."

"I sure did. But then he disappeared on us. We've had some incidents here in Boulder recently, and some of the clues made it appear as if it could have been Harland, yet we recently discovered he died in a car accident."

"Yes, that's correct. But I'm not sure how else I can help you?"

"You know, I'm not sure myself. I guess I wanted to finalize all of this for my records. I had an ex-convict reform himself, and it got me thinking. I wondered what had happened to Harland since he disappeared, and I was hoping to get some closure. Does that sound too weird?"

"Not at all. I get it. But I guarantee Harland didn't reform himself. He was wanted in connection with fourteen different fires here in Minnesota."

"I'm sorry to hear that, but it's not surprising. I understand he was involved in a chase with your guys where he went off the road and ended up in Lake Superior?"

"Yeah, it was a freezing night, January 16, 2022. My men were hot on Harland's tail when he lost control on a sharp turn, his car skidded all over the icy bridge. We kept after him, but his vehicle smashed through the guardrail and went right into Lake Superior. With those brutal temps and dangerous conditions, there was no way we could get to him in time. The car sank fast."

"Was he killed instantly?"

"I would imagine so."

"You would imagine? Don't you know? What did the autopsy show?"

There was a pause on the other end of the line. "I'm afraid there's been a misunderstanding here, Detective. We never actually found Harland's body."

"What do you mean you never found his body?"

"It was January and a record-breaking cold snap. Temperatures were running in the negative teens. It was the middle of the night. There's no way he survived. Search and Rescue performed a preliminary search of the area, but it was far too dangerous and impossible to drag the lake in those conditions. Even if Harland survived the brutal crash, he'd be dead within moments in the cold water."

"You're absolutely certain? And the body never resurfaced somewhere else?"

Tim laughed. "Have you heard of the phrase 'Lake Superior never gives up her dead?'"

"No."

"Basically, it references the idea that Lake Superior is *always* so cold that any bodies left in the frigid waters never resurface. Keep in mind, that doesn't mean that the lake is full of bodies as the internet would tell you, however it does mean that we aren't the least bit surprised that we never found a body."

I blinked, the information sinking in. "So you're telling me you assumed he didn't survive but never confirmed it?"

"I wouldn't even say we assumed he didn't make it. I assure you, he didn't. There's no way whatsoever he survived that crash," Tim said. "The impact of the crash, combined with the freezing water, would be lethal for anyone. We didn't see any signs of life, and given the risks, we had to make a judgment call."

I ran a hand through my hair, trying to process this new information. "So, for all we know, he could have somehow survived and escaped?" I knew it sounded ridiculous, but still.

"Honestly?" Tim asked.

"Yes! Of course!"

"No."

"Okay." I sighed. I was hoping somehow this could be a lead, but if the Minnesota Highway Patrol was adamant, then I should listen.

"I'm sorry I couldn't be of more help, Detective. But I promise you, Derrick Harland is dead."

"Okay, well, I appreciate the information."

"Sure thing," Tim said before hanging up.

What was wrong with me? It's like I was seeing ghosts around every corner. And what next?

When I see Sid calling me from the auto body shop, I'm still so consumed with thinking about Derrick Harland that I answered almost absent-mindedly. He must be calling to let me know Ellie's car is ready. I'll have to tell him that Braden will be dropping Ellie off instead of me. Where is Rodriguez with that background check anyway?

"Hey, Sid!" I answered.

"Hey, Howie. You said to call you if I got a black SUV in the shop?"

Huh? Oh! That's right. I almost forgot. "Are you telling me you have one?"

"Yes, but please understand I'll have to report this to the police as well. Has the perpetrator come forward?'"

"She didn't come forward, but she's been arrested."

"Oh. Okay."

Sid's halting way of talking gave me pause while the hair on the back of my neck stood up. Something was just too weird for me. "Do you mind if I stop by in person Sid?" I asked.

"Not at all. See you in a bit."

On the way to Sid's, I passed the Starlight Community Center, the parking lot was brimming with cars and I noticed wistfully how full of life it was. Children ran through the grass, splashes of water arose from the pool, and unless I'm mistaken, that's barbecue smoke wafting through the air.

Seeing everyone so carefree, I flashed back to last winter when I found Ebenita's lifeless body there. Or, more accurately, Scooby found it. And then I found that key but kept it from Detective Rodriguez. I guess I'm lucky she still speaks to me and didn't arrest me for evidence tampering. What a marked difference between then and now.

"Hey Sid, how's it going?"

"Hey, Howie. Please realize this is rather out of the ordinary and I'll need to contact the police, but since you're an old friend and it was Ellie who was involved..."

"Don't worry, they've actually identified and arrested the woman who owns this vehicle. Obviously, they'll want to send a team over to examine it and get pictures though."

"Woman?" he asked, confusion painting his face.

"Yes. Marah Sterling. I assume she brought it in yesterday?"

"Are you sure we're talking about the same vehicle?" Sid asked.

There it was again. The bad feeling I experienced when we talked earlier. "Yes?"

"Why don't I just show you," he said leading me over to a black SUV parked on the opposite side of the garage. I gritted my teeth when he pointed out the dent in the front bumper along with flecks of green paint matching Ellie's car. I walked aroud the back and sure enough there was the Green Horizons League sticker. This was definitely the car that hit Ellie. And, according to Detective Rodriguez, Marah Sterling's vehicle.

"No doubt this is the vehicle the witness saw run Ellie off the road, but you seem confused over who brought it in?"

"Yes. You're assuming a woman brought it in, but it was a young man who showed up this morning--"

"Hang on. Young man? This morning? Can you describe him?"

"Young fella. Tall. Good looking. Well dressed. Brown hair, neatly combed."

"Is his name Braden Johnson?" My mouth went dry just thinking about the possibility. Ellie could be out right now with the man who ran her off the road.

"Hmmm, let me check," Sid responded as he picked up the clipboard sitting on a tray full of tools next to the SUV. "This says a Ronald Pace brought it in."

"Ronald Pace? Who's that?"

"The man who owns the SUV, I guess? Or at least the man who brought it in."

Then it hits me. Braden isn't the only new young man I've met lately. The assistant for the detectives goes by Ronnie but I don't know his last name. And he matches Sid's description of him. Plus he would have had access to the police records. "Sid. I need you to keep this SUV here and don't let it out of your sight. No matter what. I mean it. Lock the place down if you have to!" I told him as I ran from the garage and immediately called Detective Rodriguez, but of course, her phone went straight to voicemail. Do they *ever* pick up in an emergency? "Rodriguez. Call me immediately," I told her. No need to leave specifics for now. I spun on my heel and ran back to the garage. "Sid. Do me a favor, call the Boulder Police Department, ask for Detective Rodriguez, and tell her what you just told me. Don't stop calling until you reach someone! I have to go!"

As I ran to my pickup, my mind flashed back to the first time I met Ronnie at the station when I was there to pick up Ellie. He told me he recognized her and pulled her from the crowd just for me. I remembered that it sounded unusual at the time, but it was so fleeting that I didn't realize why. How would Ronnie recognize Ellie? How did he know who she was? He knew because he ran her off the road. He knew because he was threatening me. But why? I'd never seen him before in my life until that day at the precinct. I couldn't remember when he showed up. I think it was only recently, but what do I know? I don't work there anymore. I don't remember dealing with him last December. Was he working with Sterling? And if he was working with her, why did the vehicle registration have her name on it? None of this fits like I need it to, but something has gone very, very wrong.

"Oh, thank goodness!" I declared when Detective Rodriguez' name flashed on the dashboard screen. I stabbed at the answer button, "Detective, you'll never belie--"

"Derrick Harland just walked into the police station and turned himself in," she said.

Chapter 21

"What did he say?" I asked as I quickly turned the truck to head toward the police station. No way I was missing any of this.

"I can't talk," she said, almost in a whisper. "I'll call you as soon as I can. He told the desk sergeant something like 'there won't be a key to hide when I'm done.'"

"What does that mean?"

"I have to go. Don't do anything until you hear from me."

"But wait--" was all I could say before she hung up. I have to tell her about Ronnie. She and the entire station could be in danger. *There won't be a key to hide when I'm done?* Is that what she said? Did the desk sergeant get it right? What did he...Then I knew, and a cold wave of dread washed over me. Derrick's cryptic statement clicked into place with terrifying clarity.

My heart pounded in my chest as I pieced together the puzzle. There was a bomb at the community center, hidden amidst the unsuspecting families enjoying their weekend. Panic surged through me as I made yet another sharp u-turn in the middle of the busy street, much to the annoyance of other drivers, and raced back towards the center. The cheerful, innocent scene I had passed earlier was now a literal ticking time bomb. I prayed I could get there on time, yet I was clueless about how to fix it if I did.

Derrick Harland didn't turn himself in. He got himself a front-row seat to the circus. He wanted to be there to watch it all go down. To see the discord and the devastation firsthand. It was his thing. He lived for the turmoil. He planted the bomb at the Starlight Community Center because Ronnie told him about the crucial key I found there last winter.

The fires and the nonsensical notes and running Ellie off the road were all just distractions from the real plan. And somehow Ronnie was working with him. He was feeding him information from confidential police files. He wanted us all running in circles, and we fell for it. It was all just a dramatic game for Derrick Harland's benefit. Ronnie must have forged the vehicle registration to show it was Sterling's, but he screwed up by taking his SUV to the best body shop in town. He probably figured it was safe with Marah Sterling in custody.

I stabbed at Rodriguez' number on the screen, but it went directly to voice mail. "Detective!" I shouted at the dashboard. "Derrick planted a bomb at the Starlight Community Center! I'm going there now. Your assistant Ronnie is a plant. Send backup and the bomb squad!"

As I sped down Pearl Street toward the center, my heart raced, each beat echoing the situation's urgency. The usual picturesque drive past the quaint shops and leafy trees of downtown blurred into a frantic rush; every red light and slow-moving car felt like an insurmountable obstacle.

I could almost hear the bomb ticking while my mind raced with images of families, children, and friends relaxing in the summer afternoon, blissfully unaware of the danger. I thought of them enjoying the pool, the sand volleyball, the playground, the grilled hot dogs and potato salad... Everything. They must be evacuated.

I told my dashboard to call the Starlight Community Center.

It rang twice before a young, cheery voice answered.

"Starlight Community Center, this is Shelly. How can I help you?"

"Shelly, this is retired Detective Howard O'Sullivan. You need to evacuate the center immediately," I demanded, trying to keep my voice steady. "There's a bomb somewhere on the premises, and everyone has to get out now."

There was a pause, during which I foolishly anticipated her telling me she'd do it right away, but instead, she scoffed. "Sir, calling in fake threats is not only irresponsible, it's illegal. We have a lot of people here for the afternoon, and I could call the cops on you for this."

"Yes, you *should* call the cops," I insisted, my desperation rising. "Call them now and tell them what I said. This isn't a joke."

Her tone turned icy. "I don't appreciate pranks. If you think this is funny, you're sadly mistaken." And with that, she hung up.

I stared at the dashboard, my heart sinking. I had to get there. Everyone's life at the center depended on it.

I breathed a bit easier when the Starlight Community Center finally appeared. The building was still standing, and I didn't see anyone panicking. But as I finally skidded into the parking lot, my heart sped up again, seeing the lot packed with cars and families leisurely strolling through it as if it were a normal summer day. Desperation gripped me as I laid on the horn, lowering the window to shout, "Get back! Everyone get away!" Faces turned to me with puzzled, wary looks; parents pulled their children closer, clearly thinking I was out of my mind. I steered toward the entrance, cursing under my breath, when I spotted a huge truck from the Snacks For You vending machine company blocking the way. I swerved toward the pool area instead, tires screeching as I abruptly stopped. I leaped from the truck and raced toward the pool area, the urgent need to save them driving my every step. The scent of chlorine mingled with the summer air while the laughter of children splashing and playing echoed in my ears. Strains of upbeat music pulsated from the pool speakers as I gripped the cool, unyielding, wrought iron bars surrounding the pool, shouting with all my might, "Get out! Everyone get out now!" But my voice was drowned out by their joyful din. Parents chatted, oblivious, while kids shrieked with delight, diving and cannonballing into the shimmering water. My desperation grew with each passing second. I waved my arms wildly, hoping to catch someone's eye. Every muscle in my body tensed with urgency and fear, but it was useless. A few people glanced my way, but most either couldn't hear me over the noise or simply wrote me off as some kind of drunken lunatic. I couldn't believe this was happening. Why wouldn't they listen to me?

Giving up on that, I sprinted for the main doors. Bursting into the lobby, I headed straight for the front desk, where the receptionist was alarmed but then annoyed. I must look like a jumbled mess, out of breath and panicky.

"Evacuate the center right now!" I insisted, waving my arms wildly, my voice a mix of authority and desperation. "There's a bomb!" As much as I feared causing widespread panic and a stampede, we were way beyond that. People had to get out of here.

The receptionist blinked at me angrily. Why won't she believe me? "Sir, I already told you—fake threats are a serious offense. I'm calling the cops."

"Yes!" I begged her. "Call the police! Call 911! Tell them I'm retired Detective Howard O'Sullivan, and we need a bomb squad here immediately!"

Around us, some people took notice, their murmurs growing louder as they finally picked up on my panicked voice. A man holding a little girl's hand stepped closer. "Is this true? Is there really a bomb?"

"Yes," I said, my eyes scanning the growing crowd surrounding me. "There's a bomb! Get out, get out, get out!"

That did it. The word "bomb" rippled through the lobby like a shockwave. Some faces still registered disbelief, while others showed true fear. Parents clutched their children tighter, searching in a panic for the nearest exit.

"Everyone, please!" I shouted, my voice carrying over the rising din. "Evacuate the building now!"

At that, the room erupted into anarchy. Panic quickly spread as reality sank in. Some people bolted for the exits, their faces pale with fear, while others hesitated, caught between disbelief and the growing urgency of the crowd.

Unbelievably, the receptionist only got madder. She angrily pressed buttons on the phone, but instead of calling 911, she called security, and several seconds later, a man in a security uniform ran straight for me.

"Sir!" I shouted, waving my hands to ward him off. "There's a bomb! I'm begging you. Please listen to me! Call Detective Rodriguez at the Boulder Police Department!"

"I'm calling the cops, all right. So they can lock you up," he insisted.

Thankfully, by now, most of the lobby had cleared out. Whether they believed me about the bomb or they thought *I* was dangerous, I didn't care as long as it got people to safety.

As I struggled with the security guard, who was still intent on detaining me, somehow, I spotted a boy across the lobby pounding on a vending machine. At first, it seemed odd that I would notice something like that in the moment. Why wasn't he running? Why was he wrestling with a vending machine when his life was in danger? Besides, the machine was unplugged, and the back panel was hanging open. It swayed back and forth as he continued to rattle and pound on the machine.

Next, it was like everything happened in slow motion. I glanced over my shoulder at the giant truck still parked unattended at the entrance, and it hit me. The bomb was in the vending machine! Slow motion suddenly sped up to lightning speed right before I shoved the security guard as hard as I could toward the front desk.

"Kid! Hey, kid! Get away from there!" I shouted, running full speed straight at him.

"It stole my money! This stupid machine stole my money!" the kid shouted as he continued rocking the machine to and fro.

Straining for him, I grabbed his arm, yanking him away with all my might, while his eyes widened in shock and confusion. Before he could even utter a protest, I threw us toward the nearest cover—a stairwell mere feet away.

A deafening roar filled the air. The force of the explosion was immediate and overwhelming; a powerful blast tore our world apart. Heat and debris engulfed us while a massive shockwave slammed into my back.

Pain exploded in my side as we hit the ground hard, my body serving as a shield for the boy. The world around us dissolved into a haze of noise and disarray. Then everything went black.

Chapter 22

Seconds later. Or was it minutes? Days? Where am I?

"H., wake up. Wake up now," Lisa urged.

Rats. It was Monday morning and I had to go to work. I didn't want to go to work, I wanted to sleep in today. I told her that. When I opened my eyes everything was a blur and dark and smokey. Where was Lisa? And where was my bed?

My ears rang with a deafening intensity; each pulse echoed through my skull, rendering me disoriented. The caustic smell of smoke and burning filled my nostrils, so thick and pungent it clung to the back of my throat. I struggled for each breath. The heavy air smelled of scorched metal and singed fabric, mingled with the tang of explosives, creating a noxious haze that stung my eyes. The world around me felt muted and surreal as if I were moving through a nightmare, each sensory detail assaulting me with its harsh reality.

What happened? Wait! It was a bomb! And there was a boy. Where was the boy? Where were all the people? Are they screaming? I couldn't tell. What was that infernal ringing in my ears? My mind was awhirl, and I couldn't think straight.

Where did the boy go? I searched frantically, only to discover him sprawled out next to me on the cold hard floor. Oh no! Oh no! Please let him be okay! My own body ached with the impact while blood trickled from my forehead, but there was no time to assess the damage. "Hey! Hey! Talk to me, buddy! Are you okay?" I shouted, still sounding like I was in a tunnel.

The boy was trembling, but he looked mostly okay. "What happened?" he mumbled.

"There's been an accident," I told him. "Don't move while I get help."

"I think you landed on me," he said.

"Stay here," I repeated.

I tried to get up, but the floor tilted beneath me. "Whoa," I mumbled, dropping to my knees. I'm terrified to think of how many people must have been critically injured or worse. This was all my fault. Why didn't I think of this before? The signs were there. I had to get to the people. So many people. All those families at the pool. I had to help them. The police and fire department must be on their way, but it would take them a while to get here.

I continued trying to drag myself out from under the stairwell, but it was so hard and so painful. Everything hurt. One more deep breath led to another coughing fit and a sharp pain in my left side, but just as I gathered the energy to attempt to stand again, I heard a voice cutting through the pandemonium.

"Detective O'Sullivan! Howie! Are you in here?" Detective Rodriguez' voice, clear yet filled with a raw, desperate urgency, rang out. The sound of her voice calling my name brought a surge of relief, a lifeline in the midst of the devastation. I coughed, trying to clear my throat, and shouted back as loudly as I could, "Over here! We're over here!"

Detective Rodriguez peered around the stairwell. "Oh, thank the heavens!" she exclaimed. "He's here!" she shouted over her shoulder. "Two gurneys!"

"No, no," I protested. "Don't waste one on me. Just the boy. Help the others who are hurt. I hit my head, but I think I'll be okay."

"Others? What others?" Rodriguez asked.

"They're all dead?" I stuttered on the verge of weeping.

"Dead? Howie, they're all okay because of you."

"But the explosion."

"Yes, but thankfully for us, Derrick placed it in a vending machine that sat against a concrete-reinforced wall. You two took the worst of it. Well, the lobby of the community center will be closed for a while. But don't worry; I'm sure they'll fix it before the next Pedals of Promise Event," she said, half-jokingly, referencing the charity project I lead here every year at Christmas.

How could she be joking at a time like this? She was just trying to make me feel better, right? "But what about the receptionist? She was right there," I stammered.

"When she saw you shove the security guard, she realized you were serious, so she helped the guard hide behind the desk with her. You were smart to dive underneath the stairs. You saved this boy's life and numerous others because you cleared the lobby."

I listened in stunned silence as Detective Rodriguez continued to explain that, miraculously, there had been no catastrophic injuries from the bomb. Relief washed over me while I still found it hard to grasp that such a powerful explosion hadn't resulted in any deaths. My mind replayed the chaotic scenes, the intense heat and force of the blast, the deafening noise. I had braced myself for the worst, expecting the aftermath to be filled with tragedy. Yet, here we were, with everyone accounted for and no life-threatening injuries. A fact that seemed almost too good to be true.

"Detective O'Sullivan!" Rodriguez' sharp rebuke startled me from my thoughts. "Let the paramedics help you!"

I continued to resist the paramedics trying to place me on the stretcher, my frustration boiling over. "I'm fine," I insisted, though every breath sent a sharp pain through my side. One of the paramedics, a young woman with determined eyes, met my gaze firmly. "Sir, you hit your head, likely have cracked ribs, and could have internal injuries. You need to be checked out." Her calm, professional tone clashed with my stubbornness, but the concern in her eyes gave me pause. Despite my protest, the realization of my injuries was sinking in, and I reluctantly allowed them to guide me onto the stretcher, the adrenaline slowly giving way to pain.

"I'm going with you," Detective Rodriguez insisted as they wheeled me through the lobby.

As the paramedics rolled me outside, I was confused by the sound of cheering and applause that greeted us. The crowd, a sea of relieved and grateful faces, clapped and shouted with fervor. For a moment, I was confused, unable to comprehend who they were celebrating. My eyes searched the crowd, looking for a clue, until Detective Rodriguez leaned down and whispered, "That's for you, Howie."

The realization hit me like a wave while a mix of humility and gratitude swelled within me. Despite my injuries and the chaos, these people saw me as a protector, someone who had faced the danger head-on for their safety. But to me, running toward danger was just something I did out of instinct. I never had to think about whether I should. I just did it.

"Ellie! Does Ellie know?" I asked, the moment the ambulance pulled out of the parking lot, heading to the hospital. The last thing I needed was to freak out my granddaughter.

"Ellie is meeting us at the hospital. And you need to calm down," Rodriguez insisted while the EMT nodded her head.

"Derrick is still in custody, isn't he? Please tell me he didn't escape!"

"He is. And after this, he obviously won't ever leave prison. The receptionist told us you were the one who knew the bomb was in the vending machine."

"I tried to park at the entrance, but the snack truck was there. Derrick obviously came in disguised as the snack guy and planted the bomb. When I saw that boy at the vending machine, I realized that's where it was. I grabbed him and dove under the stairs."

"And before that, you cleared everyone out of the lobby," she reminded me.

"If that blast had gone through the wall into the pool area..." I started.

"It didn't, Detective. That's the important part," Rodriguez scolded. "Had Derrick placed that bomb in almost any other part of the building, there's no telling what could have happened.

Ronnie! I almost forgot! "Ronnie! He's a plant!" I started to get worked up again.

"Control yourself, Detective. We know. I got your voicemail. He's Derrick Harland's second cousin. They've been plotting this ever since Derrick was declared dead."

"And the cashier who claimed Sterling bought all that lighter fluid?"

"Paid off. By the way, you owe your friend Sid a case of beer. Before I had the chance to listen to your email, he showed up at the station and raised such a ruckus we nearly arrested him. When he told us about Ronnie's SUV, I pulled up your voicemail."

"Where is he now?"

"Oh, we got him at the bus station buying a ticket and trying to flee."

Phew. I finally began to relax a bit. I didn't want to think about how close we all came to everything ending in a disaster.

"You want to know the best news?" Detective Rodriguez asked.

"Yes?" I responded, my brain still fuzzy. Derrick and his cousin were going to jail. I no longer had to worry about Ellie being attacked by my enemies. The community was safe. What else is there?

"The mayor reinstated the festival!" Rodriguez exclaimed, grinning down at me.

Chapter 23

While the sun started to set on the 100th anniversary of the 4th of July Festival, I strolled through the crowded park with Detective Rodriguez, basking in the ongoing and joyful sounds of celebration. Despite the community spending the entire day here, the party was still going strong, and everyone got their second wind in anticipation of the fireworks show. Children darted past us in swirls of red, white, and blue, their laughter rising above the hum of conversation as the park finally got much-needed relief from the hot July sun. The air was still thick with the aroma of sizzling hot dogs and sweet cotton candy. It took me back to simpler times, and I loved every minute of it.

I watched families spread out on blankets enjoying their picnics, couples strolling hand in hand, and older folks like myself walking about with content smiles, soaking in the live band's patriotic tunes. It felt surreal that just the other day, the security of all these happy people had hung by a thread, one we had managed to stitch up just in time.

I turned to Detective Rodriguez, who watched the crowd with a satisfied yet vigilant gaze. "We did good, Laura," I said, my voice carrying a weight of relief.

She nodded, her eyes softening for a moment. "Yes, we did, Howie. Thanks to you."

"You want to know a secret?"

"Sure."

"Part of it was pure dumb luck."

"Don't sell yourself short, Detective. You may be retired, but you're as sharp as ever."

"Okay, yeah, I'll give you that one," I laughed. "I can't believe how fast the festival came back together."

"We owe a big thanks to Kara Belmont for this," Rodriguez reminded me.

"I agree. She really came through for us in the end."

Once Detective Rodriguez had Derrick Harland securely locked away, and she learned that everyone survived the bombing, mostly unscathed, she called the mayor and demanded he reinstate the festival. When he complained there wasn't enough time to get the word out, she immediately called Kara and insisted the news station broadcast it far and wide. While I spent the day in the hospital recovering, under doctor's orders, the town showed up en masse to put everything back together. It was amazing.

As we continued our patrol of the park, I felt the vibrancy of life around me more acutely than ever. As truly grateful as I was to be here and have the Derrick mess behind us, my heart ached when I thought about how ecstatic Lisa would have been that the festival went on better than ever. She would have been soaking up every second of the scenery: kids tugging at the hands of their parents to get to the next stall, the scent of popcorn mixed with the earthy smell of summer grass, the bursts of laughter from teenagers trying their luck at the carnival games—all so vivid, so alive.

Earlier, when I watched the pie-eating contest, a little boy, his face smeared with blueberry pie, looked up at his cheering parents, his eyes sparkling with the thrill of messy victory. It was moments like those, simple and pure, that we had worked to protect. The thought made me smile, and a genuine contentment spread through my chest.

Eventually, Sammy joined us, yet another hot dog in hand. "How many have you eaten?" I asked.

"I lost track after five," he explained. When I laughed at him, his expression grew thoughtful. "You ever think about all the normal days we fight for, Howie? All the little things that add up to a life?"

I returned his smile and followed his gaze after two children ran by waving glow sticks.

"Sometimes," I confessed. "Especially today. Hey, have you seen Jack?"

"Last time I saw him, he was flirting with the gal who runs the kettle corn stand."

"Good for him." I laughed.

Derrick Harland's apprehension played back in my mind. Knowing he was behind bars and finally answering for his crimes provided a closure I hadn't realized I'd needed. It wasn't just about proving I was right; it was about affirming that no shadow, however dark, should ever be allowed to fall over these simple joys, these communal celebrations of life.

We wandered over to where Ellie had a massive blanket laid out for all of us to enjoy the fireworks, but just as I approached her, a familiar-looking young man walked up to her first, holding two glasses of lemonade, and handed her one.

"Hello, Mr. O'Sullivan," he said.

"Hello?" Who is this guy, and how does he know my name?

"Gramps, you remember Braden from the crash scene, right?"

Ugh. It's the paramedic who was making goo-goo eyes at my granddaughter.

"Hello," I responded more forcefully this time while trying to give him my most intimidating stare. Not sure how I felt about my granddaughter dating a first responder. Yeah, yeah, I know, irony, right? But why couldn't she find herself a nice accountant or a chef? How fun would that be? A chef in the family. Oh, well.

Before I could dwell on it any longer, my grumpy thoughts were interrupted by the mayor announcing over the loudspeaker that we should all rise for the National Anthem. But as the singer stepped up to the microphone, Scooby, who had been sleeping in the wagon I'd been carting him around in, sat up, ears perked. Uh oh. As the first few notes rang out, Scooby let out a prolonged, accompanying howl, throwing his head back dramatically, much to the amusement of the nearby onlookers. My cheeks flushed as more heads turned our way. Scooby, sensing that he was gaining attention, howled even louder. Thankfully, instead of complaining, the crowd around us chuckled and applauded his impromptu accompaniment.

We stood together as a community, hands over hearts or hats held against chests. The singer's voice soared over the field, a touching reminder of how resilient our community was. Scooby, still not one to give up attention, continued his canine rendition until the last line was sung, prompting a wave of laughter and applause from the amused spectators.

Once the anthem ended, a cheer erupted from the crowd, and the sky lit up with fireworks, painting the dusk with brilliant colors, while a collective "ooh" rose from the crowd.

Tonight, as bright lights danced across the night sky, reflecting in the wide eyes of children and the tear-filled eyes of their elders, I felt a chapter close and a new one begin. With Harland behind bars, the community could breathe easier.

"Happy 4th of July, Gramps," Ellie said, her voice mixing with the crescendo of fireworks.

"Happy 4th of July, Ellie," I replied, my heart full, watching the sky blaze with freedom's colors, knowing we had done well, not just for ourselves but for this small, vibrant slice of America. Life would go on here in Boulder, and so would we, ready for whatever came next under the broad and watchful sky.

After the fireworks, we moved the party to the Veteran's Hearth Bar for a final drink, and I raised my glass for a toast, addressing Sammy, Jack, and Ellie. "After all we've been through this week, Scooby and I are taking a well-deserved break," I announced, a smile spreading across my face. "We're headed to Lake Tahoe for a week of fishing. I've rented a houseboat, just me, the dog, and the open water." My friends' faces lit up with genuine happiness, and I felt a lightness I hadn't experienced in days; the thought of the crisp lake air and the quiet solitude of the water was already washing over me, promising a peaceful retreat from the havoc we had endured. From here on out, it was nothing but my relaxing retirement...

Is Howie really and truly retired? Probably not!

Copyright 2024 by Author B I Skinner. All rights reserved.

No part of this publication may be reproduced, distributed or transmitted in any form or by any means, including photocopying, recording, or other electronic or mechanical methods, without the prior written permission of the publisher, except in the case of brief quotations embodied in critical reviews and certain other noncommercial uses permitted by copyright law.

Note: This is a work of fiction. Names, characters, places, and incidents are a product of the author's imagination. Locales and public names are sometimes used for atmospheric purposes. Any resemblance to actual people, living or dead, or to businesses, companies, events, institutions, or locales is completely coincidental.

Cover design by B I Skinner

More Books by B I Skinner

Ghostly Glenwood Mysteries Paranormal Cozy Mysteries

The Case of the Haunted Hotel

The Case of the Pilfering Poltergeist

The Case of the Poached Peridot

The Case of the Gym Ghost

The Peach Cobbler Caper

The Case of the Haunted Radio Station

Spooky Shanty Realty Mysteries

Afterlife in the Attic

The Lifeless Listing (coming in August)

Holiday Cozy Mysteries (non-paranormal)

Sleigh Bells & Sleuthing

Fireworks & Felons

Marcall's Breakfast Cafe Paranormal Cozy Mysteries

An Eggscellent Day for Murder

24 Carrot Caper

Daggers and Donuts

Cupcakes and Corpses

A Crime of Cranberry

Peppermints & Pandemonium

Star Spangled Homicide

Blood Curdling Ballots

Sign up for my email list here

https://mailchi.mp/9ebce0da866a/email-signup-list

Visit my website

biskinnerauthor.com

Follow me on Instagram **@bethiskinner** Facebook **@biskinnerauthor**

www.ingramcontent.com/pod-product-compliance
Lightning Source LLC
Chambersburg PA
CBHW060540160726
47991CB00001B/409